**Root
Leaf
Flower
Fruit**

Root
Leaf
Flower
Fruit

Bill Nelson

TE HERENGA WAKA
UNIVERSITY PRESS

Te Herenga Waka University Press
Victoria University of Wellington
PO Box 600 Wellington
teherengawakapress.co.nz

ISBN 9781776921164

A catalogue record is available from
the National Library of New Zealand.

Written and published with the support of a grant from

ARTS COUNCIL OF NEW ZEALAND *TOI AOTEAROA*

Printed in Singapore by Markono Print Media Pte Ltd

for Fern and Jarvis

Contents

Root

Still the taste of mud. Clay, soil, half-decayed
leaves, pine needles, earth. Gritty, metallic,
even after washing my mouth, soda water,
toothpaste. Foaming, frothing. I can still taste it.
Everywhere. Rammed into the mouth and ears,
nostrils, hair, beneath the fingernails,
caulking the throat. Like the trees, the roots,
the mud. Sending a message.
Designed to look like an accident.
But no memory of what happened.
I might as well be someone else.
No message.
Then again, there was foreboding –
the afternoon before, a storm rolling in,
Latika on the phone. *I'll be home late.*

It sounds horrible out there, she says, her concern
reinforced by the rain and darkness
already wetting the windows. And I remember
reassuring, placating, and also, worried myself,
considering briefly, to let my friend down,
go home. And then she's gone. Or at least
the memory of her is gone.
And it could have almost happened that way.
And now, I don't know anything for sure.
The world is different but I can't say
in what way, like someone moved all the furniture
and now I'm tiptoeing around, expecting
to crack my shins on a coffee table.
But I'm here. Drifting in. Waking up.
In hospital. More than once. Mud everywhere.
Torn clothes. Injuries. *Where am I?*
Waking up. Mud. *What happened?* She's there,
definitely there. Answering politely, over and over.
How long have I been here?
And then, *I bet it was spectacular.*
Trying to make her smile. A curtain
around the bed ripples like a flag.
The shape of something
large and angular. With elbows.
Corners and elbows. I roll my head
and pain shoots up my neck.
She's not smiling
and I ask if I've said all this before.

Alternating feet, I loop through the neighbourhood,
arriving where I began, the roundabout, always
a roundabout, and then another, gentle,
calm, grassy, filled with shrubs and
reassuring trees. The cars evacuated. Dry rectangles
of asphalt where they once waited, dormant,
heavy and unpopular. The people gone too,
the air somehow harder to push through,
and I shuffle towards Somerville Road
the long way, a pedestrian path, following
drainage channels, a concrete culvert snaking
through the neighbourhood, and beyond,
the life of swings and slides, patchy
grass, a pool collecting leaves.
I've come to like not going anywhere: every street
pretty much like the last, footpaths separated
from the road, a grass verge, tastefully planted
traffic islands, into pedestrian crossings, into
cul-de-sacs, into quiet turning areas, into carparks,
into leafy trees. And the front yards
like display cabinets with ornaments and glassware,
carefully placed and beautiful but without
practical function, except, perhaps, as an invitation
to stay away, fences, walls, wrought iron.
My head throbs so I stop
and try to remember everything I see
so I can recall it later, like a photo, like a journal,
but I can't do that and the sun is too bright
so I shut my eyes; the white silhouette

of the treeline
burns into my eyelids.

The last time I saw my grandmother I was turning
thirty-one. It was the day after my grandfather's funeral.
I sat next to her in the foyer of a care facility
for stroke survivors. Mum had gone into the office
to sign the will documents. She didn't know what was in them,
she didn't even know they had a will. Not unusual
for my mother to not really care about things like that.
And maybe she was now the owner of the farm.
Or of a set of teaspoons, and my uncle, the oldest
and the only son, making off with the land,
or maybe my aunty, the baby – still the baby –
but more likely, I thought, my grandfather
would want it split between them, fairly, evenly,
hoping it would bring them closer together.
My grandmother didn't register my presence.
Didn't make a sound or look at me or the other residents.
She didn't acknowledge the nurses when they smiled at us.
Her eyes roved but didn't settle on any particular thing.
We never talked much before the stroke. I was too young
and she was too serious. And since the stroke,
there was nothing much to miss. She'd had bursts
of vitriol or self-loathing for a few years, but these
were rarely directed at me, mostly at my grandfather
and my uncle and aunty. And in the last few years,
even those had subsided. Mum said
my grandmother was finally coming to terms with her situation,
as if she was midway through a thirteen-step programme,

finally moving on to step six. But it felt less like
rehab, more like a slow decay. Into what?
I didn't know, but I didn't share my mother's kind fatalism.
Maybe my grandmother was a vessel, a cracked cup
that we all filled with our own ideas.
Maybe it was me who was in slow decay.
Maybe her life had begun again.
Maybe she had left us behind, a side step
to the left, maybe she was free,
freer than she'd ever been
to do, to say
whatever she felt like.

Latika is repairing a wind-up watch
on the kitchen table, the tiny pieces
dismantled and arranged carefully on a rubber mat,
and next to her a set of tiny screwdrivers,
assorted tweezers, small pots of liquid
and some neatly folded paper towels.
How was the walk? she asks without looking up.
I take a bottle of milk from the fridge.
The physio took pains to explain, *Four weeks,*
at least, maybe more, months, years, maybe never.
I'm not sure what's supposed to change.
I feel the same, more or less,
maybe a little less smothered,
that under-duvet feeling, dulled
sounds, distant voices, but how am I
supposed to know if that's normal
or not,

if that's how it's always been?
I take out two mugs, pour the tea.

He'll tell you it's because the kids were into it.
She always says this
at dinner parties, right after someone laughs
and says, aren't you a bit old to be riding a bike?
And they usually laugh and the conversation ends there
although it continues on in my head, through dessert,
through the extra glass of wine that we don't want,
through the ride home in the taxi, through my toothbrush,
through to the other side, into my dream, where everyone's laughing
and I'm shrugging, but I can't shrug enough to make them stop,
and I slip out the back, slip on my helmet and kneepads,
slip on the overpriced BMX shoes that I bought last year,
dab a few drops of oil on the chain, check the tyre pressure,
and pedal up the hill to the BMX track. I can still hear
the laughing so I stop to visualise the jumps in front of me,
what I need to do, the tricky one with the lip that kicks up
at the last minute. And I keep at it as I start my favourite
playlist – the '1993 mixtape', in honour of a tape I made
as a lonely thirteen-year-old, listening to the radio
in my bedroom late at night, frantically hitting record
when something in the intro – a drum beat, a bass line,
something in the undercarriage – struck me as mixtape worthy.
No edits, no rewinds. One take. Whatever comes, stays.
I found the tape years later and was impressed by how good it was –
eclectic, a mixture of obscure and popular,
old and new, global and local.
And as I roll away and pump the first corner, gathering speed,

the chirpy bassline of 'Walk on the Wild Side' rolls with me.
Its contradiction of fairies and plums, hustle and hairy legs.
I hit the first table top, my front wheel lifts,
my back wheel leaves the ground –
I'm suspended, nothing more for me to do
except enjoy the relief of the setup,
the ellipsis, the timing, a weightless feeling,
a shift of body weight fore and aft,
pushing down, then pulling up
all in one smooth movement, speed,
but also deliberation, like a river,
deep and dark and quick.

Twenty years ago, the houses around here
emerged from the landscape almost overnight.
One minute paddocks and swamp, the next
a suburban utopia. Although maybe it took decades.
The area bare or under construction
in my high school years, starting probably
before I arrived, but it's still there, that image
of the farms behind the school, swampland
and scrub, abandoned, no animals to speak of.
I remember running cross-country under duress,
splashing through the puddles, walking
the last few kilometres, talking as we clambered over stiles
and then linking up with the new boulevard
and the semi-constructed pedestrian walkways.
I remember finding a stash of porn under a bush, possibly
from the eighties, judging by the art direction and body hair,
and how no one would believe where I'd found it,

and later, lying on the grass with a friend, smoking
a badly rolled joint and pretending we were stoned.
And like background noise, the grumbling of the families
who had been here for years, in every house,
at every chance meeting on the corner,
or down by the dairy, walking the dog on the beach,
rage, assumption, the assumption of rage, everyone
becoming a foreigner, an intruder, before their eyes.
And then as I grew up, school friends, friends of friends,
cousins, aunties, grandparents, the children
of the grumblers, they were the ones mortgaged up
next door, buying themselves into the future,
doubling the floor area, halving the land, putting in
porticos, split windows, flagstones and barbecue areas,
triple garages, ready-made lawns.
They were the ones who moved to this foreign land,
who made it their own,
who found they couldn't leave.

The kids are downstairs making a fort. A sprawling
percale shanty town. *Let me help* I say, tucking the blanket
between the mattress and the base. Giggles.
Telling me to come in, so I lie on my back
with my head through the door.
The fort is almost complete, soft toys lined up, the youngest
feeding them felt sausages and the oldest piling pillows
on top of a blanket to hold it down, stepping back
to admire her architectural skill.
Suddenly I don't feel so heavy. Tired. Yes. Bored. Yes.
A little resentful. Maybe. But also

like I'm perched on the fulcrum of a seesaw,
and the kids, one on each end are doing all the pushing
and I'm just here to slow things down a little.

Ten more minutes I say, a meaningless number,
a meaningless unit. But through repetition
they've come to know what I mean. *Two*
the youngest says. He thinks he's buying himself
time. I slip out the door and into the bathroom.
A shower, hot water on the nape of the neck,
vanilla and honeysuckle shower gel, peppermint
toothpaste, 48-hour deodorant, Borneo rainforest.
I like to go to bed clean.
I wonder if this is the best way.
As if this one thing represents everything
that has gone wrong in my life, as if it affects
everything I do, everything I am, everything
that will happen from now on. What would life
be like if I got up and showered in the morning?
Like everyone else I know? Like, what would happen
if I started the day clean instead of half-asleep?
I spend a long time watching the steam glisten
against the glass, form into drops and cascade
down the door. I haven't shaved for days
but my razor is on the other side of the bathroom
on the windowsill, too far to reach without
spilling water all over the floor, so I pick up Latika's razor.
Paddle-like and pink. It's always been there,
suction-cupped to the wall, and I realise
I've never touched it before.

I tuck the youngest in first, and then the oldest; always
the same routine, the same order, and I wonder
if that hierarchy will always exist,
if we've created that or if it runs deeper, some biological order.
They're allowed to choose two books, but it always
turns into three. Today it's *A Lion in the Meadow*,
the page with the dragon that I know scares the youngest,
but also that he can't wait to see, the yellow eyes,
smoking nostrils, and the jet of fire from the mouth.
It's the only image with no words, covering two pages,
filling the whole space, literally an act of imagination.
After that, it's the book form of some TV cartoon series
with superhero animals, and then a few nursery rhymes
that we can all recite by heart. They wriggle
and try to get out of bed and I gently usher them
back and close the door and eventually
the force of their tiredness drags them into sleep.
Their tiny bodies are almost perfectly still,
mouths agape. Both ugly and beautiful.
And I can't help but think how uncluttered they are,
how for them, consciousness is an open question,
a thing still flowering. And for me, it's something
inescapable, even in sleep. I go to bed myself
and fall asleep with the light on. In the morning
the sour taste of gritted teeth, worn enamel,
crops gone to seed.

For a few years all they did was scrape topsoil,
erasing, levelling, flattening. Then they built

retaining walls and flood banks, culverts and drains.
And roads, wide, curvaceous, shining and black,
painted lines, white concrete footpaths, dropped kerbs
and channels for the driveways that would eventually arrive.
Then they added street lights, electrical cabinets, slender
trees, staked, caged, tied together. And then
nothing else happened, for years
it was left to bake in the sun,
the dirt so thick and dry even weeds wouldn't grow.
It looked like a scale model
in a Tim Burton film, kitsch and fake.
And then the four-wheel drives arrived, architects,
engineers, surveyors, builders, plumbers, electricians,
plasterers and painters. Supplies were delivered,
stakes driven in, concrete slabs were poured,
timber framing erected. First one house, then another.
Like foals finding their feet, they stood uncertainly,
and then with more confidence; the pace accelerated.
On the next street, another, and another,
the empty sections filling fast, more houses,
framing into roofing, roofing into walls, walls
into windows, doors and trim, knobs and latches,
paint, polystyrene, plastic, brass numbers.
And then footpaths, garages, driveways and fences.
And finally, when the builders were gone,
new topsoil was raked in, trees and shrubs, grass
rolled out like a carpet and, right on cue, the owners.
You could tell from the lights on at night and the newly leased
cars parked in the driveways. And we all said
how ugly and new it was, talked about the way

it used to be, about the time we searched for four-leaf
clover in the field, the whole day in the sunshine,
climbing back over fences, testing for electricity with a stick.
And that sunshine, that endless summer sunshine.
And we all agreed it was good not to be living
in a construction zone anymore, that horrible clay,
unfinished structures, spent building materials.
It wasn't good for our collective mental health.
And now we don't talk about that much,
it doesn't come up, and you wouldn't know by looking at it
that the earth was once scraped raw,
terraformed, and the surface of what was there
is now only a few centimetres beneath our feet.

The research group has organised a morning tea
but no one wants to make a speech,
so we just eat, drink coffee and go back to our desks.
The head of department smiles at me sympathetically
as I leave the room and climb the ladder to the observatory.
All glass and metal, a domed hothouse. There hasn't
been an observation made here in years.
My desk is up a couple of steps where the machinery
for rotating the telescope used to be, half hidden
behind a bookcase of old journals.
When I first arrived at the department,
young and enthusiastic, it was different.
Up here in the old observatory,
we were a little enclave of misfits – postdocs
like me, master's students, technicians,
anyone who didn't earn an office downstairs.

A PhD student from Norway decided to grow chillies
and tomatoes. They seemed to multiply
as the summer wore on, growing higher
and higher. We had to sweep aside a jungle of vines
to get to our desks. Even now I can smell
tomato leaves and ripening fruit.

A few years ago, the new Computer Science annex
opened up. Café-style work spaces,
ping-pong, whitewashed plywood, natural light.
And there was no one up in the observatory,
just me and my laptop, tapping away. The ladder,
the glass dome, the sweltering heat, the icy cold.
My little observatory with nothing in particular
to observe.

I open my laptop and the screen blips into life
like it's only been a few minutes since I was last here.
I'm surprised how easy it is to get back into it.
The commands come like muscle memory, although
not really in the muscle, I suppose – somewhere deeper,
like turning on a tap, like that banging of pipes
under the house. Or maybe it was always easy,
like reciting the alphabet,
like any six-year-old could do. Sometimes
I wonder how I got here. What if
I hadn't chosen Canberra to do my PhD?
What if I had taken that year off?
What if I had gone to art school instead?
But the truth is I love processing data.

I love how ugly it can be, how the biggest problems
are always overcome by breaking them down.
That's where the real science is, I like to say to people.
And if they don't look impressed
I tell them that I'm studying hydrogen molecules
in deep space and, if that fails, *how it may help us
to predict climate change, although not directly,
a component, you could say.*
And then I make a joke. Science funding, manipulation
of the system, academia, politics, the media, the role
of science in our society, and they say things like *I bet Einstein
didn't have to worry about that.*
Meaning Einstein the genius, not Einstein the amateur physicist,
or Einstein the father, or Einstein the patent examiner,
or Einstein the incestuous philanderer, or
Einstein the campaigner for nuclear disarmament.
Einstein didn't have it so easy either, I say.
At lunch, one of the professors sits briefly at my table.
*I know your funding is almost up and you've been off
for a while, but I hope you're not going to work too hard.*
I tell him I wouldn't dream of it.

After work I walk to the shopping mall, or plaza as it has recently
been rebranded. A few quiet shops, gift cards,
a coffee chain, Auckland's last suburban post shop.
I'm there for the moderately sized supermarket
tacked on the side. I wobble through the food court
and select a basket with wheels and an extendable handle.
I buy rolled oats, snaplock bags, and a packet of Dark
Chocolate Wheatens. The checkout operator says *Hi*

but doesn't look up and I pay in cash. Outside
I feel dizzy and take a seat in the bus stop,
almost no one is around, no shoppers exiting
or entering, a few cars, but that's it.
Above me, in the corner of the carpark, a large
four-posted sign with slanted green script –
MEADOWLANDS SHOPPING PLAZA.
I wonder who came up with the name.
What did they think was so meadow-like,
so plaza-like about the place? Below the sign –
Countdown
Unichem
123 Dollar Store
Bodyzone Physiotherapy
And below that, a tarpaulin banner –
ALL THE MAKINGS OF A HIDDEN GEM.
I stand, still a little woozy, but able to manage.
Concentrating on something else helps and I examine the lines
on the palm of my hand and then find a point
in the distance. An exercise the physio suggested
and the only one I remember to do.
The Meadowlands roundabout, far away
but near enough – small, attainable, circular.
I start walking towards it.

The last, last time I saw my grandmother
I was twenty-four and about to start a PhD in Australia.
I had been working as a software tester at a company
that made electronic fish finders. My job was simple:
Push button X, then Y, then power off, then button X again,

then Y again. Repeat but start with Y instead of X.
Repeat but end with X instead of Y. Repeat that
but start with Y and end with X. Do something
unexpected. The script didn't say that, but often
I did push random buttons. Then I'd log the bugs, attend
a defect review meeting, argue with the developers.
One day I quit and emailed my MA supervisor
to ask if anyone they knew needed PhD students.

The day before I was due to leave for Australia
my mother invited me over for dinner.
My grandmother was there, and my grandfather of course,
as well as my brother and his new girlfriend.
I was the first person in the family to go to university,
and my grandmother was celebrating.
She told my grandfather to go fuck himself,
threw a fork across the table, and finally, after dessert,
told my brother's girlfriend her neck was too fat
for her head, or was it her head was too small
for her neck. The girlfriend tried to laugh
and my grandmother growled like a dog.
My mother apologised several times.
My grandfather made his excuses and wheeled her out the door.
I helped him lift her into the car
and watched them drive away. Just before
they went round the corner, she looked out
the window and flashed me a little grin.

The phone in the hallway rings. I know it's Mum
before I answer. The hallway phone is always Mum.

Your grandmother has had another stroke.
She's never one to panic, even when my father
was in a car accident, when we went tramping
and got lost and it rained and the rivers spilled over
and we couldn't cross the valley to get out.
Can you call your brother? she says.
This time I can hear the panic in her breath
and I spend too long considering what to say.
Actually, don't worry. I'll do it, she says.
Or maybe you should do it. No. I'll do it.
Okay, Mum, whatever you want, I manage to get out
before she hangs up. I drink a large glass of water,
something I've been trying to do lately, and sit down
on the hard kitchen floor, my back against the cupboard
with the rubbish bin and cleaning products inside it.

We gather in the emergency department waiting room.
Parents, uncles, aunties, cousins, cousins' kids,
cousins' partners, old bowling buddies,
neighbours, some other people I've never met,
and my own family, quiet in the corner,
sitting in a row, evenly spaced. Everyone present.
Except, of course, my grandmother, in a room
down the hall. Near death, perhaps.
The doctors don't really know. Continuous tests.
What's going on inside her. What's going on
inside her brain. Can we operate. Is there anything
left to operate on. She's near. Just down the hall.
We can't see her yet. What is she near to.
Small groups, talking, murmuring,

someone rolls out an old anecdote,
a polite laugh, some nodding, silence.
My uncle approaches through the crowd,
the eldest, reluctant responsibility.
I offer my sympathies and he says thanks
and that he's surprised to hear I've gone back to work.
Yeah, I'm not sure how long I'll last, I say. *You know, science, funding.*
The uncle nods. Smiles. There's something he can't quite say.
He glances towards the window. *The farm's*
looking at bit dejected, he says. I've heard
that the garden, once perfectly kept, is now overgrown
and unkempt, the paddocks covered in weeds,
vines growing over the house.
We're thinking we'll have to sell. He sounds
neither glad nor upset. *There'll be costs.*
And I was wondering. He interrupts himself
by lifting his teacup to his lips and gulping loudly.
I was wondering if you'd like to help tidy the place up,
get it ready for sale. Might, you know, do you some good.

We decide to go for a family bike ride – me
riding solo, the youngest perched
on a seat on Latika's handlebars,
and the oldest pedalling her own bike, twenty metres
behind, no matter the speed, twenty metres,
like she's attached with a tow rope, within sight
but distant. And like this, stopping
and starting, strung out like a military patrol,
we sweep the streets, progress slowly
through the undergrowth of the suburb.

Latika is somewhere ahead
and stops to wait for us, her torso twisted,
one hand on a handlebar and one on the saddle.
Yesterday, she asked if I was ready to get back on my bike
and I said, *Yeah, sure. No. I mean. Yes.* And now,
even at a sedate family pace,
the seat feels too high off the ground, the bike
more skittish than I remember, but I'm determined
to do this. The thought of staying at home,
imprisoned by a distance I can walk, is a thought
I don't want to have anymore. So on we pedal
until the oldest is too tired to go any further.

I stand up to absorb the shock of the kerb through my knees.
The front tyre skitters as it strikes the sharp edge
and for a moment I imagine it sliding out,
my reactions too slow, and I go down,
hitting the concrete with a crunch
and the the oldest has to watch
and realise for the first time
that her parents aren't invincible
that they are soft and primitive
like jellyfish. But that doesn't happen.
I'm okay. Nothing happened. I carry on.
We're almost at the shops! Latika yells from ahead.

The next morning I wake at two then go out walking.
Just after the accident, I slept all day. I couldn't read
or watch TV. The dull ache in my head
kept relatively quiet in the upstairs room, the warmth

of the bed. But recently I've struggled to sleep, even at night.
I have the streets to myself, at this hour
no one else is up, they work long hours, so many things to do,
no time to be up in the middle of the night.
I was like that too, every minute of every day, busy
with something else, I often couldn't find the time
to have a shower or cut my fingernails.

I walk past the mall and end up paused
in front of a clothing shop, the mannequins
dressed in muted garments, large hats and handbags.
And right in front, a mannequin in an evening gown,
halter neck, floor-length teal silk wound round a slim waist.
I wonder what it would feel like, that fabric,
stretched over my collarbones, bare at the back,
tight against my stomach, draping over the hips, tumbling
to my ankles. A car suddenly appears,
a racing engine, headlights sweep over the roundabout
and flash across the window. My shadow rears up
over the display and I can see the dress
is cheaply made, an ugly colour, the hem rippled and bunched.
I take the delivery driveway at the back of the shopping centre
then turn right onto Clydesdale Avenue, a slow walk up the hill
towards home. I hear the same engine, louder, turning the corner,
chomping through the gears, headlights again.
The engine slows to a deep burble and the car crawls
a few metres behind me. I can feel eyes watching.
I quicken my pace, the car quickens too, the crossed shadows
of my body stretch out in front of me and I begin to jog
lightly, leaning forward, elbows high,

like any other suburban jogger in their daily routine.
A couple of hundred metres to the house,
at least two corners. There's no one around,
no lights on, no other cars, no walkers. Now wishing to see
another person, any person, the very thing
I've been trying to avoid. I consider darting down
a random driveway and knocking on the door, hoping
someone is home, but suddenly the engine whines
and the tyres rip into the tarmac and a shout cuts the air.
Fuck off faggot! The car accelerates past me
and I dive onto the grass verge
in what seems like, even as I am mid-air, an overreaction.
But as I sit on my bum, the wet grass already seeping
through my pyjamas, I see a projectile loping
end over end towards me
like a satellite making its way across the sky.
I watch it glint in the fractured street light, watch it
drop toward me, growing in size as it gets closer,
and then it explodes on the footpath
right where I had been standing.
Beer flowers across the concrete and pieces of glass scatter
like diamonds. The car's tyres
groan as it leans heavily and disappears round a corner.
For a full five minutes after it is out of sight,
I can hear it. I trace its course
through the neighbourhood, through the roundabout,
down Millhouse Drive,
chopping down through the gears and accelerating quickly
at the Cascades traffic lights. Locals, then –
locals who know the shortcuts and back streets.

I probably know them, or their parents,
or their cousins, or their cousins' parents.
Almost as quickly as they arrived, they're gone.
The street back to how it was.

It was the strip of dirt down the side of the house that sold me.
I had visions of replicating my cousin's potato patch,
her lines of strawberries, fava beans, heirloom tomatoes.
Oh the bounty! With just a little effort from me in spring
and a water every few days, food would grow before my eyes.
Seeds into seedlings, seedlings into plants, plants into shrubs,
flowers, fruit, beans, nuts, tubers. Within a few months
I could watch the wonder of nature take over, leave me
to cheer it on from the sidelines. I'd be growing something
and it would taste like home, like dried soil crusted
on potato skin, beans from the stalk, plucked and juicy,
tossed straight into a salad. That's what sold me, that's why
we wanted to move here, why we don't have an apartment
in the city. Of course, there were other reasons – the price,
the kids, the car, the noise – but I think I would have dug in
much more if it wasn't for that thin patch of soil
that took me three years to discover was in fact nothing.
That I was no gardener, I couldn't even grow a daisy
let alone produce what you could reasonably call a vegetable.

There's nothing underneath, you see, said an elderly neighbour
one day as I was forking up plants to find a handful
of fingernail-sized potatoes. *You plant the plants
in the topsoil but it's what underneath that counts.
And they stripped it all away.* She looked upwards, like

she was talking to someone in the sky. *You might as well*
plant your potatoes in rocks. Then she smiled and said
I've got some lovely Red Russets from a friend
if you want some. I said thanks but no thanks, and pulled out
all the plants in one go, an attempt to make at least
one meal out of all this hard work. And that night
we each had a spoonful of potato salad to go with the rest
of the ingredients we bought from the supermarket.

What will you do out there? Latika says
while I'm writing a resignation letter.
At first, I'd thought it was a stupid idea
but the more it sat with me
the less stupid it became.
Clear air, hard work, no one else
to expect things from, to expect things from me.
Maybe it will do me some good? I parrot.
There's nothing wrong with you, she says.
One of the kids screams a scream of torture from the hallway,
and I can hear the other one sneaking away,
the tiny patter of bare feet on carpet.
I just need my old self back, I say.
I don't know whether to sign off
with 'Yours sincerely', 'All the best', or 'Cheers'.

I wake with sleep in my eyes. Small organisms
floating over the cornea, swimming up toward
the eyebrows. I blink and push them back down
but they resume their ascent. I blink again
and they glow in the morning sun. I name them,

each recognisable by the way he, she or they move.
I give them childhoods as well as genders,
and university educations, a first love, pet hates.
The morning drifts away. I realise the sun is high in the sky.
Latika has left me to sleep. This makes me sad,
that I'm not much use anymore,
and my eyes are wet again, just briefly,
but enough to wash away the sleep. I blink
and wipe my cheek, peel the duvet back
and head to the kitchen for toast and coffee.

The phone in the hallway again.
She's stable, Mum says, *though not communicating.*
They say all they can do now is monitor her.
But they won't really say what they are monitoring.
Just monitoring. Brain activity I guess.
Like they think she might be a vegetable.
I don't think anyone uses that word anymore, I tell Mum.
She asks if I want to visit. *I'd like to,* I say,
but I'm trying to get an article finished
before I leave. I don't really want to work
while I'm on the farm. I shouldn't work
without funding. It undermines everything.
We all wish it didn't but it does. Too many people,
half my team, all working from home, no funding,
no prospects of funding. A lot of enthusiasm.
Not much else and even the enthusiasm's
running out. I can tell she's not listening.
I can hear her gasping, like she's running out of oxygen.

We agree that Latika and the kids will go with her
and I'll try to make it.

I climb the ladder to the observatory for the final time.
Today it's hot, perhaps the hottest
we've had in years; condensation is already running
down the glass walls and accumulating in small puddles.
I gather up piles of paper and throw them in a cardboard box.
I'll sort through them later. I scoop up my laptop
and place it in the box, wind the cables around my hand
and throw them in too. I wonder if I should tidy
the other junk lying around,
then realise, even after all these years, none of it
is mine and I don't even know whose it is, like
it could have been here before I arrived, perhaps
before the person before me, the person before them.
So I decide to leave it and slump in my chair,
a few final half-hearted spins. I'm not sure
what I should do for the rest of the morning.
My feet are fidgeting like I've had too much coffee,
but also like I need even more coffee.
I could go to the lunchroom and see if anyone's around.
There's certainly no one here to talk to. There hasn't been
for a while.

Latika is packing my bag for me.
She's never done that before.
Meticulous in how she packs her own bag,
everything in mesh holdalls,
but usually she couldn't care less

about my own untidy habits
as long as they don't affect her.
She chooses too many collared shirts.
I'll never wear them on a farm.
I need T-shirts, shorts, woollen socks.
Or that's what I imagine I'll need.
She rolls up eight pairs of colour-coded business socks.
I know she's not happy a lot of the time,
but this isn't a lot of the time, it's a short time,
a very specific time. The kids give me a hug
and scamper away, no different
than if I was going to work or out for milk.
She kisses me and both our lips are dry.
I get into the car and lower the window.
She asks me to call when I get there.
I can see something about to come out,
but I know she doesn't want it to come out
so I don't wait for it. *I will*, I say and, *I love you.*
She says, *I love you too.*

The last last last time I saw my grandmother was yesterday.
A face in the dark blot of the ceiling, in the middle
of the night. I woke up and her face
was floating above me and my heart was beating hard.
And I couldn't get back to sleep.
I didn't try to put it in context, didn't try to remember
if I did actually wake up or if I was still asleep,
I didn't ask Latika if she remembered me
gently rattling her awake to ask if she could see her too.
One day at a time, they say. Which always sounds

a little condescending. But then again
maybe it's fine not to worry about the future
or the past. Eat, sleep, dream, eat, sleep
and wake up, probably still dreaming.

As a child, the vortex of the farm. School holidays.
Mum was working. A vortex of boredom
and physical work, and being outside, and waking up
and just getting on with it, and no one else for miles,
glasses of milk, congealing porridge, bread
and butter pudding, and the smell of dirt
in everything, consuming everything,
even though you leave your gumboots
at the door, scrub your hands with industrial-strength
detergent and shed your clothes into the laundry basket,
it's like it has entered you, like iodine,
like no matter how hard you try, a yellow stain
that won't shift. As a child, remembering,
as an adult.
Not sure who is who, which is which.

Leaf

Why don't you go out there, we can talk
when you get back. I could tell that Latika partly
wanted me to say no. Partly I wanted to.
She'd have to look after the kids, work
five days a week, pick them up, drop them off,
make dinner, bathe them, milk, stories, bedtime,
up again, back to bed. Then she might have an hour
or two, and then up again at six to start all over,
and all I'd have to do was tidy up a farm,
do a bit of research at night to keep things ticking over,
no whining demands from kids
who don't understand wait, or soon, or later.
I could see she was waiting for me to protest,
at least, somewhat, and like I said, I wanted to
but then nothing was said and in the end,
nothing was lost.

A poster with squares bordering each day, loose line drawings of rhubarb and crescent moons and ancient wisdom, she checks it in the morning, eating her gruel, drinking her nettle tea, humming and thinking, *there's nothing to be done*, she says, or *things are looking up,* depending on the symbols, the colour-coded squares, she marks off where the seasons align, the summer has been too warm, the bees yet to arrive, she takes a builder's pencil tied to a piece of string and marks the days – bar, bar, bar, bar, slash – that's five without rain, there is still time, there are still three weeks if the wind cools and it rains, just a little, tomorrow she will trim a wind break, a leaf day, then there's the spinach, for the autumn crop, and the tractor, a concession for her husband who could never live without a machine to work on, is on the blocks, holed up in the shed, red and black parts neatly arranged on the floor, *I'll have it working by Tuesday*, he says, ideally they wouldn't have a tractor, the diesel, steel and rubber, spilling gases, but it's a concession, for her husband, and everything of value is a concession, by Tuesday, *that's enough time*, she thinks, she marks that on the calendar, next to a drawing of a straw hat, and drops the pencil, swinging from its string in a dark grey semicircle, on the wallpaper below.

The crunch of gravel under rubber, wrestling
with the wheel, cresting the hill – blue sky,
treetops, house, a heavy body coming to rest.
I pull up on the handbrake, twisted
Mintie wrappers swim in the well.
And then the silence floods in, and the boredom
I remember so well, and even inside the airlock

of the car I can hear the solemn dining-room clock,
hear the dark rooms, the dust particles,
that odour of rubber boots, dirt and wingback chairs.
And the paddocks are drier than I remember, the grass
browner, like the moisture has been sucked out
and what's left could blow away
if anyone wanted it to. I open the door
and the silence breaks, a soft drone, insects
in the distance, doing whatever it is
insects do, and for now I decide to leave
the luggage in the car.

I scuff the rows of dirt with my foot,
hardened and cracked like old leather.
Ploughed long ago, mounds, tiny pyramids,
rising half-hearted above the weeds.
A lack of rain, a lack of care, and the sun
beating down, down on my skull,
through my skull, my eye sockets,
cheeks, neck, skipping the brain,
straight to the nerve endings, a spread of warmth
in my fingertips and the soles of my feet.
The field is not abandoned. Depleted
but restorable. Connected. My feet.
With a little help. Did I say that out loud?
I'm not sure. There didn't seem to be any sound
but it feels like someone said it.
I trudge back to the farmhouse,
kick off my boots and start work.
I need somewhere to sleep, eat,

and maybe to wash. And that painting.
The girl with black eyes, overly large head,
a field of colourful flowers, her bare knees,
clutching, haunted by something,
perhaps, or at least, indifferent.
That will have to go. Before I do
anything else I gently lift the painting off its hook
and slide it into a cupboard. No one will notice.
The only trace, a slightly less faded
rectangle of wallpaper.

As a young woman, she lost a bet with her best friend and
became a hat model, tall and lean, with a long nose and red
lips, you never saw her eyes, just the lower half of her face, the
hard lines, lips, jaw, cheekbone, the local hat shop in Gisborne
did their own catalogues back then, she hated advertising, but
she was young and beautiful and saw no reason not to let her
hair down, or put it up for that matter, the best way to show the
unusually long curve of her neck, when she angled her head
in a particular way, the hardest part, getting that line right,
but when you did, it was magnificent, unlike her husband who
didn't like lines, preferred fuzzy shapes in the half light, in
the morning before the curtains were open, when she felt him
watching her, just for a moment, before he would roll over and
switch on the radio, he was never a model, although handsome
in a foundational sort of way, like brickwork, like when she
first met him at a dance, his thick mechanic's hands, black
smudges on the back of her dress, marks that would never
come out, never let her down, and try as she might, she can
barely recall those days, the dark shadow of youth, a phrase she

may have read somewhere, or may have made up, she writes it down in her diary anyway, the phrase and the question as to its originality, the same diary she would try to burn later, fearing her husband would read it, and he would relay the information to his mother, and the words would take on a life of their own, one she could no longer control, and she wrote down intimate details of their sex lives, orgasms, dates and duration, in between, the cycles of the farm, what needed to be planted, harvested, and then she lit it with a match, believing she was burning the person she used to be, not realising that paper, stacked and deprived of oxygen, doesn't burn.

Unpacking my clothes, I find a diary in the wardrobe,
and then another, and then a whole stack.
Some with burred covers and edges. No dates,
no titles, no names. But judging by the yellowing pages,
at least twenty years old. Inside,
my grandmother's handwriting,
cursive, elaborate, flowing unbroken across the page.
The words beautiful but difficult to read
until my brain, or my eye, adjusts,
like walking into a darkened room.
And then I realise it's written in the third person:
She planted the first of the shelter belts today.
Her hands have turned red from the soil.
She misses the ocean.
I try reading it in the first person.
I planted the first of the shelter belts today.
My hands have turned red from the soil.
I miss the ocean.

I slam the diary shut and push it back
into the cupboard. I leave my clothes
half in, half out of the suitcase.

She was twelve when the war started, she loved to watch
the newsreels from the National Film Unit, mostly the
boys building railroads or people at home converting tyre
packaging into bandages, but then regularly the warnings,
the rising sun, a map with red arrows curving down through
the Pacific, missing Australia and coming straight for New
Zealand, she was never quite sure but she thought she saw that
arrow pointing at Gisborne, where the invasion would begin,
in a BBC accent, imprisonment, beatings, death, it couldn't be
worse than school they joked, where they listened to the siren,
were shown a muddy track into the hills, an orange forestry
hut, six berths for eleven kids, and at playtime, sandwiches and
whispers, secrets and half-believed half-truths.

I take out my laptop, rummage around for the power cord,
and make some coffee while I wait for it to warm up.
I look up the farm on Google Maps. Aka Aka Road,
down the big hill and halfway up the other side.
From a satellite, I can see the extent. Smaller
than I remember, old pine trees to the north,
a driveway bending around the south and east,
and on the west side, the creek my grandfather
dammed, choked with watercress and eels.
On all sides then, surrounded.
But I can zoom out and see the suburbs creeping closer.
Pukekohe, Waiuku, Patumāhoe. Where once

there were other farms, now it's cul-de-sacs
and avenues, some with infrastructure already in place,
the houses yet to be built, but footpaths and smooth tarmac,
driveways leading to plots of dirt and weeds.
But mostly I notice the shadows of the street lights,
reaching across the road, no doubt shiny and new, unlit.
And when I look up from the screen it's dark outside.
I flick on a tasselled floor lamp and rummage around
in the cupboards. Noodles, rice, pasta,
a can of kidney beans. I find some chilli powder
and throw a handful into the pot of beans.
I sit down with a bowl, a spoon and a mug of water
and open my email. Nothing. Scroll down. Nothing.
For three months, no email from an actual person.
Just receipts for online purchases, warnings
about my overdue library books,
bank statements, new logins from unusual devices.
Nothing real.

When they first talked about retiring, it was going to be flowers,
long rows, tropical and temperate, mountainous and wild, she'd
always loved the idea of farming flowers, but the research had
done her in, it seemed there was no way to make it work without
pesticide, herbicide, fertiliser, without doming everything
in plastic and glass, so their plans changed; vegetables, eggs
and honey, and later, avocado trees, growing food, organic,
Demeter, Bio-gro, and the WWOOFers – Germans and Brits,
backpackers and drifters, but also Brazilians and Swedes and
the odd Korean or Japanese kid, some keen on organics, some
just looking for a place to stay, most leaving grateful, some

leaving with money from the cash box or a jar or two of honey, and she wasn't bothered; it was fate, flawless young people doing flawed things, but her husband didn't think that way, bad decisions haunted him, he could have made more money, taken more efficient routes; he couldn't stand people who made stupid decisions, was never shy to criticise, just like their children, one foot in the old world, free love and marriage, making money and getting stoned, they couldn't understand why you would wait so long to do something you loved so much, but she couldn't blame them, the husbands, the children, the drifters all just trying to find a comfortable position to live in.

The organ has stacked keyboards, bakelite switches
and backlit buttons. I play it after dinner.
I remember playing it as a kid, mainly
messing around with the automatic drum tracks.
I was always drawn to bossa nova, that weird instrument
that sounds like a baboon, and now
the smooth weight of the keys, and the foot pedals
with an even deeper heft, and I struggle
to remember how to make chords and instead
play long religious notes until I start to put myself to sleep.
When I'm finished, I depress the power button
and the lights slowly dim, an endless hum
from somewhere inside the heavy woodwork.

She started with windbreaks and compost and only then ploughed the fields, a lot of earth to move, that's when the WWOOFers came in handy – heavy lifting and digging, too finicky for the tractor, they came and went, sometimes only

for a few days, which was almost more trouble that it was
worth, but she enjoyed them all, their optimism and lack of
care, the cultures and backgrounds so different from her own,
combined into an easy soup of laughter and wide-eyed wonder,
something she had once although could barely remember it,
her children, marriage, wiping out everything that she was
before, some became friends, some were like children to fret
over, penniless and hopeful, she watched them growing out of
the earth, not unlike seedlings she thought, taking something
from the farm but also replenishing it, replenishing her, and
when they left she felt more in love than ever, and tried to
hang on to the feeling.

I lie on the creaky steel-sprung bed and pile
the heavy blankets on top of me. The ceiling is high
and worn, like it's been scrubbed free of paint,
the grey boards showing through.
Once as a child I woke to click beetles dropping
from that ceiling. I panicked, screamed,
and she rushed into the room, turned on the light
and like magic, all the beetles disappeared.
She tucked me back in and left me
lying in the dark with my eyes open.
But mostly I remember her from photos,
lean arms, collared sleeveless blouses,
looking straight into the camera. Which was not
who she became. Once, my grandfather forgot
their wedding anniversary – he was lost
in some contraption he'd dredged up –
and she scrubbed away at the benches all night,

grinding away the surface, millimetre
by millimetre.

I make a list. I'll work
outwards – start in the hallway, then the dining room;
I'll throw away the fishing magazines, the piles
of old newspapers, some published
before I was born. I'll scrub the kitchen,
dust the lounge. The bedrooms
will have to suffer. The laundry aired out.
And I'll water-blast the mould from the verandah,
trim the lawn, tidy the flower beds
and prune the trees, rake the stones in the driveway
and pluck weeds out with my fingers, tidy the garage,
remove the junk and old tyres from the rafters.
I'll top the hedge around the house,
then the paddocks, turn the soil, hide
the weeds, dig in the compost. It seems
pointless but the compost piles need to go
and I can't think of anywhere else to put them.
I'll whack around the avocado trees,
throw the dead fruit in a pile, repair the torn
plastic in the hot house, throw out
the dried-up tomato plants. I'll slap
some paint on the letterbox. The first thing they'll see
of course. Prospective buyers,
the investment of their life. An impression
radiating inward, towards that little muscle,
decisive, deep in the stomach.

It happened when she was alone, while her husband was visiting his sister in Napier, she woke to find one of the WWOOFers next to the bed, naked, on his knees, praying and mumbling, something in German, or Polish, he stood and wailed, scrambled at the quilt, she yelled, flicked on the lamp and she could see his eyes, black and glossy, he jumped on the bed and she bucked her legs, hit him on the side of the head with her knuckles, a dull thud, and he fell, crashing into the dresser, she called for Bernie, knowing he wasn't there but thought it might frighten the guy off, he stood and walked calmly out of the room, she could hear him repeating something as he walked down the hallway and out the back toward the worker's cabin, she locked all the doors and windows, called 111, she wished she had some way to contact her husband and get him back here, she tried Margaret but there was no answer, the urge to leave and make a run for it, over the hill to the next farm, she hid in the bathroom and locked the door, and after what seemed like hours the police arrived, a strange metallic voice she didn't recognise, and after a search they found him, lying in the furrows of the field he had helped plough the day before, raving, his body plastered with dark red soil, smeared everywhere like shit, over his eyes, his biceps, his stomach, his penis, his feet, smeared over him, rich, red and deep, like beetroot and chocolate, like wine and shit.

My body argues with itself. I've never wanted sleep
so much, but first, eat and shower, then sleep.
I lie on the floorboards in my underwear.
The ropes in my back spasm and then relax.
In the hallway, the spine of the house, I trace the line

on the ceiling with my eyes, the part
where the house was split open, transported here
from up north. Still fresh, raw and torn
as the day it was cut in two. I can see where the jamb
was split, where they had to cut a wall in half,
and presumably there's a line under my back
too. I can remember the house with its insides
exposed, squatting in the dark on the backs
of two trucks, and then flanked by utes,
the swivelling orange lights as the house set off
for the motorway. Later, it planted its feet
in the bare levelled earth, a verandah twirled like a cape,
the garage grew into a comfortable second lounge,
and eventually a driveway appeared, a lawn,
trees and shrubs that grew into a shelter belt, but the scar
remained, unplastered, unpainted, still as torn and rough
as the day it was sawn, a reminder perhaps of its
not-so-northern past, or maybe my grandparents
planned, one day, to split it again in half,
load it back onto trucks and lurch off
to some other destination. And as I lie there,
the day ebbs away and I wonder if I should buy sandpaper
and ceiling paint, if the buyers will even think
to look up, if I will need plaster or would that crack,
if I should use something with silicon in it. And then
I'm awake, morning light under the door frame.
A rooster, somewhere, giving it everything.

The field wintered with covering crops, oats and rye and lupin,
and in the spring, the soil rich and fertile, her husband turned

it with the tractor, digging in the stalks and roots and withering leaves, and when she lifted a sod, worms wriggled and dripped from her hands, as her husband worked behind her preparing the seeder, and after, she made dandelion lemonade and they sat on the verandah, their backs aching, dried dirt caked on their foreheads, under the fingernails and behind the knees, the taste of it in the mouths, and then her husband said it was time to book the WWOOFers they needed and she said nothing, watched the snapdragons and lavender and borage and honeysuckle, their arrangement edging the lawn but not in straight lines, curved and meandering, small enclaves to wait in, paths to wander down, a sanctuary from the industry of the farm, and it looked like her mother-in-law's, except all her flowers were edible, could be made into salads or tea, and that pleased her, no waste, everything farm, the farm everything. *Okay*, said her husband, *we'll manage.*

In the wardrobe I find cylindrical boxes,
some large, some small, some even smaller.
And inside all of them, hats. Hats with brims,
hats with feathers, veils, ribbons, bows and brooches.
Most of them dark and opulent but some lighter
like a shallow pool or a leaf. I turn them around
in my hands. And I can't resist –
I place one on my head, and in the mirror,
except for the colour, I could almost pull it off –
Terry Pratchett, Orson Welles. But no, it's no good,
my ears are too fleshy, pink rubber frisbees.
I need something that balances that out. I try another
and another. I try all of them. And then in the back

in an old teal hat box,
a rounded disk of felt, smooth, soft, shocking pink.
I try it on and adjust it slant, like an old movie heroine.
I pull the veil down like a visor, and in the mirror
behind smoky mesh, one eye,
a hint of jaw and cheekbone, pouted lip, and finally
my nose, long and thin, elegant, like they always said
it would become, a beautiful nose, that could have been hers.

Her list of tasks thumped like a drum, sudden and back-breaking; no one ever told her it would be such work, but she never shied, everything hard, her childhood, getting married, having children, running the garage, the restaurant, the time she was ill on, literally, a bad apple, the time she was alone for months while her husband was away and she withered in a flat in Birkenhead, pity glances from her children, no one told her life would be like this, every muscle in your body aching, making lists every night, waking every morning, wandering around in the middle of day, doing things, no idea what you are doing.

I've barely dented the list, the farm
is nowhere near tidy, and next week an agent, a valuation,
but it'll have to do. I'll do what little I can
between now and then and it'll have to do.
I pull out a large pigweed, careful to grab it low
and pinch out the roots, but the stem snaps near the surface
and I throw it on the pile. I turn round and see the hedge
choked in pink flowers and heart-shaped leaves.
The book I found on a bookshelf says it's morning glory,

almost impossible to be rid of, but it comes away easily
in my hands, and in a few minutes I have a huge pile
of tangled vines. I wonder why it's called morning glory,
which makes me think of the other meaning and I laugh
out loud, the sound swallowed up in the distance to anyone
who might be able to hear it and suddenly I can hear my own
blood pumping, and it rushes and swirls inside my head,
and perspective suddenly zooms away like in *Vertigo*,
and closing my eyes makes no difference, and I'm still
zooming away, zooming out of body, out of the world,
and I can see myself in the distance, frozen, tiny,
further and further away, and I have to sit down
and take deep breaths and concentrate
on my body. Breathe. Move. Chest, hands, fingers.
I get up and walk around, and then, just like that
it's gone.

Her husband went on his trip the year the last of the children
left home, he wanted to do a tour around Europe with his
mother, this was before grandchildren, before the farm,
before she'd learn about biodynamics and holistic health, so
she moved to a flat in Birkenhead, read Russian novels because
they took a long time and walked to the dairy to buy bread
and milk, though eventually she stopped eating and drank
tea all day, and her children fretted, *He'll be back, it's just a
holiday* and *Do you want to come with me to the Coromandel?* but
she didn't, she just wanted to be alone, and she'd heard that his
mother had written to one of the kids, told them to keep an eye
out, male callers, suspicious phone calls, she felt like sleeping
with someone just to teach him a lesson, her son brought a

bag of apples, and she could see the pain on his face, having to look after his mother, *Thanks dear*, she said, thinking about *Anna Karenina*, the book she'd finished yesterday and was still thinking about and hadn't thought about her husband at all, and she took a bite from a glossy red apple, the inside floury and bitter, and then without pausing took another bite, and another until only the core was left and then she ate the core, the seeds, and stalk, and licked her fingers, even though there was no juice on her fingers.

Blisters on my hands.
I soak them in ice water,
apply Savlon and plasters
which loosen and slip
when I do the dishes.
I give up and leave them
undressed as I work
and they turn dark brown,
calloused and lumpy,
protection, dirt and skin,
iron and carbon.

And a few months after the stroke, the children and grand-children came to stay on the farm like they used to, sitting around the table, eating quickly, slurping soup, tearing into bread, *Can we watch TV?* the oldest grandchild said, and the others followed him, as silent as ants, and her husband was left to shovel soup into her puckered mouth while the children watched on, batting him away, *No, no more*, but he persisted, always persisted, hovering the spoon above the bowl until she was ready, and later, lifted her into the bath, awkward, although he can feel that she is becoming lighter, like paper, and he refuses his children's help, he can manage on his own, and he learned to cook, macaroni cheese, stir fry, the secret he tells his children over and over, like a scratched record, a little chicken stock, a little splash of steam right near the end, that's what makes it so delicious.

The agent. A slim grey suit, his ankles showing,
white shirt, neatly parted hair,
I specialise in niche properties, he says.
Don't worry too much about the garden,
people like a project. He flicks his hand,
without looking, toward the fields. *The soil*
is what people are here for. Put that
out front. He presses a card
firmly into my hand.

Last week she heard her husband on the phone dismissing the carer, and she rolled her eyes. *Don't tell me you're not happy,* he said, *you called her a bitch and an f'ing c-word, I can't deal with that anymore,* but she liked doing that, screaming and swearing, it felt good, but she could see that he felt bad so that he had to let the carer go, and now he felt bad that he felt good when she was gone, as if he enjoyed the pain, the struggle, an old hermit with a sick wife, holed up, locked in, and now after dinner he reads her the paper, avoiding the stories about road deaths and child violence, and when he accidentally starts to read one about a baby tortured by its parents, her whole body curls up, he notices and puts the paper aside, *How about we go for a walk to the top paddock*, he says, she doesn't answer and he lifts her quietly into the wheelchair, her head lolls to the side, she is getting lighter all the time, she can feel that too, how he seems able to lift her with less effort, like with every step she takes closer to death he's getting stronger, younger, here in the top paddock, where the soil is hidden by weeds, where she remembers all the work she did, the aching and the dirt and falling into a deep sleep after, waking renewed and fertile, and now, the field overgrown, magnificent, luscious weeds reaching for the sky, fuelled by beautiful soil.

The roller door slaps loudly against the stops
and I fumble for the light switch. Neon tubes
flicker and then catch, and there it is,
squat and industrial, green mudguards, green wheels,
green engine cover, KUBOTA embossed proudly
on the side. Smaller than I remember.
At eight years old, climbing it, struggling
to reach the first step, pulling the levers, pushing pedals,
buttons, dials, no idea what they did.
I search old boxes of mechanic's tools, heavy and worn,
rifle through a cupboard, a box of pamphlets.
Manuals. One for the tractor, a couple for classic cars.
I flip past the safety warnings, the specifications,
straight to 'Getting Started'. The brake pedals,
one for the left wheels, one for the right,
clutch and gears, throttle lever, speed-lock lever,
emergency brake, others to operate the attachments,
and lastly how to slide the seat forward.
The keys in the ignition. I wiggle the gear lever

turn the key – preheat – start.
Nothing, no whine, no stutter.
A page on jump-starting.
I nose the car into the garage and open the engine cover.
I connect the leads and leave the car running.
I turn the key, again, nothing. The manual, nothing.
I get out my phone and start typing, *tractors for noobs*,
tractors for beginners, *Kubota tractor won't start*,
and finally, *Kubota B6100 won't start*,
tractorbynet.com, eight pages of replies.
The clutch pedal needs to be pressed. I try again,
the engine turns, a slow raspy bark, over and over,
and finally, a chug of life, but then a splutter, a spit,
a fading hiss, and then it dies.

After the farm really started to hum, they planted the avocado trees and waited for them to fruit, the promise of exports to Australia, great prices, the same promise made in Australia, the fruit sailing gleefully across the Tasman, passing a ship carrying fruit the other way, everyone making money then losing it the next day, under pressure from the banks, a drive to export, the APA, ENZA, HNZ, Turners and Growers, eventually they bowed out and sold everything at the Franklin market, direct to restaurants, fruit shops, no safety net, like walking the top of a fence like when she was girl, arms out, toes pointed, like an Olympic gymnast, stopping next to a plum tree, nestling into its mossy branches, drunk on soft fruit.

I try the hats again. A beret, a stripy sunhat,
a fascinator. I dip into her dresses, calf-length,

stripes, floral, thin and light, like wearing
a parachute. Slacks, a silk blouse, pearls, clip-on
earrings, thin bracelets, and then nylons,
rolling them up like in the movies, unfurling
over calves, bony knees, the hair on my shins
like seaweed on a beach. And I plough on,
the bottom field, the top field, brittle soil corkscrewing
over the shiny blades, furrows, broken and exposed.
I can feel her approval, a job well done, finally
doing something useful, and as I look behind me
to admire my handiwork, I can also feel silk
twisting effortlessly around my waist.

Doing things right, no pesticides, no fertilisers, organic and
beautiful, no poisons to enter the body, she read more – self-
sustenance, biodynamics, permaculture, no-dig farming –
and applied for Demeter certification, but she never thought
she'd take it so far, burying chicken bones in the garden,
making potions, planting by the phases of the moon and the
constellations, making everything by hand, compost, seedlings,
natural sprays, and her body the same, exercise, aerobics, the
rebounder, vitamins, magnesium and iron, vegetarianism,
which almost everyone disapproved of – *You're getting so thin*
and *You're working too hard*, and the meditation, that drove them
mad, but she felt so good, her days long and overlapping, like
woven flax, like a mat, like a basket.

I shut off the Kubota engine, slide the earmuffs
up to my temples and take another look behind me.
In a few days, the agent and potential buyers

will arrive to inspect the farm.
And on display, the soil, turned, broken,
still rich and dark red, although at this time of year
a little pale and dry. But it's done, and the rain is coming,
I've seen it on the news, over the Tasman.
The timing couldn't be better. I wish
the sky would open up right now, right here,
like in the movies, without warning, my hair and dress
stuck flat to my body, and me squinting into the heavens.
But it's never like that. In real life the cloud has been
thickening all day, slowly, predictably.
The rain is supposed to continue for days, the kind
that only a farmer could love, or an unfunded physicist
wanting to do some reading and plug a few leaks
before he has to go home.

It congeals, wanders upward, a chock in the cerebellum,
jammed in thin arteries, thickening, cells, starved and in
panic, chucking it in, spreading like the crack of a fresh sheet:
the cerebrum, the limbic, motion, speech, memory, systems of
contingency, non-existence, a simple misunderstanding, who
was doing what, who would dial 111, who would wait, *If we'd
seen her earlier*, he's seen her his entire life, full frontal, messy,
failing, succeeding, nerves under attack, hospital corners like
an iron maiden, and on Sundays a deep coma, unrecognisable,
her sleep face, like bitter chocolate, the reassuring beep you
hear in the movies is bullshit, it's the first thing they turn off,
and then the worm, the screen, the warning lights, the print-
outs, all that's left is an alarm, a decision they tell her husband
he needs to make before it's triggered.

Only when I see the bike – the brake cables
ripped off, a broken light, the front wheel
buckled like a Pringle, pine needles
jammed between the tyre and the rim,
and the helmet, weirdly, without a scratch
does it come back to me. Or if not back,
at least bubbling up. And it sharpens.
Back to work, friends, coffee, Latika,
playing with the kids, and only when
there's no one else around, a feeling
that something's not right,
that something has changed,
that it's impossible to know.

The day before the stroke, she slipped into her gumboots and out the back door, tested the soil, foliates, pH balance, ground old bones, roots and fish scales, sprayed it on the recently turned earth, some ingredients bought in, not everything had to come from the farm, but ideally, yes, a closed system, no input greater than the output, closed, like the biodomes in Siberia and Arizona, and that terrible movie with Pauly Shore, but the idea still interesting, the perfect organism, but not perfect, like science, perfect like learning from mistakes, like testing soil moisture by rubbing it between your fingers, getting hot, she donned a straw hat and headed to the avocado orchard, the soil there too rich for avocados and the investment, immense, they won't see a crop for three years, *It's the way of the future* she told her husband and he nodded, pleased at the word *future*, she could see the bank account in his brain filling up, *The avocados will be huge, you'll see,* the

thrill of a sure thing, they discussed later how long it takes
for avocado to fruit, and his bank account drained a little,
easy money, avocados were not easy but it was too late now,
they were planted, committed, *When you invest time in somethin'*,
she'd heard her husband saying those exact words to the
grandchildren, their sunburned faces and squinty eyes, and
he was right, neither of them could let the avocados go, *It's*
heaven or bust as her mother used to say, picking that phrase
up from the American soldiers who trained in Gisborne, twin
lines jogging down the beach, shirts off, combat trousers and
black boots, dark chests and thick stomachs, *Heaven or bust*
she thought, pulling a leaf off an avocado tree and mashing
her thumb into its waxy skin, releasing that familiar odour of
aniseed and salt.

The rain arrives, starting slowly, just enough
to dampen things, and then, by evening, 'setting in',
heavier and heavier, until there's no air left,
only sheets of water, the air
like background noise. Tucked up inside the house
in the pyjamas Latika gave me for my fortieth birthday,
I watch the rain through the window, the rain gauge,
nailed to a post, filling up and then overflowing.
And as I open the first journal article, the latest results
published by my research group, my name conspicuously
absent from the list of authors, a drop of water
splashes onto the varnish of the dining-room table,
then another, and after a moment, another.
I look up and see a bead of water growing
on the edge of the light shade. In the kitchen,

I choose the largest pot, place it under the drip.
The metallic clang annoying at first but after a while
it shifts to the gentle plop of water hitting water.
I read a few more pages of the article, taking notes
in a small book I bought for the purpose, then I notice
another drop near the door darkening a patch of carpet.
And then another in the hallway, in the bathroom,
several in the spare bedroom. I put away
my reading and spend the rest of the night
emptying pots and bowls, running out of bowls,
finding a cupboard full of preserving jars,
using those, the big ones and then the little
chutney jars, emptying the bowls and pots
and jars, all night and into the morning.
And by the time the rain finally stops
and the dripping slows to a manageable level
I'm too tired to read academic articles
and I roll into bed, pull the covers over my head.

She cared for her body like the farm, fertilised, fed, washed
and prepared, watered and wintered, minerals and vitamins,
pills and potions, left to relax, fallow, days of the week,
months of the year, the moon, the seasons, she buries cow's
horns stuffed with manure, skulls, intestines and bladders,
manure and quartz, peat and dandelion, yarrow, stinging
nettle, valerian and horsetail, no poisons, no chemicals, and
in the autumn she retrieves the horns and scatters the dust
on the field, turns the rest into compost, she pops a shot glass
full of pills, swallows them with nettle tea, the neighbours,
and her family say nothing, directly, but she can hear their

voices in the night, *hocus, fairy dust, where's the science*, they
worry that she doesn't eat enough, but they all take a box
of vegetables, they all wither away on their own, with their
instant coffee and their pesticides and their gro-magic instant
lawn, and they worry about her mind too, her well-being, how
can she continue, after that scare, so isolating, but she doesn't
care, still doesn't lock the doors at night, still doesn't turn on
the pager her husband bought for her after he returned from
Europe.

In the afternoon I wake groggy and steamy,
make a cup of coffee and go outside
to inspect the farm. In the top field, the furrows
are gouged out by the rain, all the soil
washed down the hill, collecting in fans
and driven up against fence posts and tree trunks.
Leaves and twigs blanketing whatever is left,
blown across from the shelter belts.
A few windbreak trees lean over, out of line.
Their roots lifted, ripped from the ground.
I trudge up to the bottom paddock, unlatch
the gate and stop.
A large muddy lake stretches across the grass,
all the way to the fence on the other side.
The grass blades prick through at the edges,
but in the middle it's deeper, at least a foot I guess.
It'll take days for it to drain. And on the other side
two of the fences that I've just mended are broken,
branches leaning heavily on the wire, buckling
the posts and splintering several of the battens.

I latch the gate shut, flick the cold dregs of coffee
into the bushes and walk back to the house
to make myself another one.

Flower

Then there was the collapsed lung.
Or so they said. I'm glad I don't remember it,
don't remember the feeling of not
being able to breathe,
the air sucked out of me, my brain,
the medulla, that automatic part, trying to do
what it's done since the day I was born
and not being able to, failing spectacularly,
and the thinking part of me
not helping either. Latika told me
I gasped and wheezed
and as she walked into the hospital room
that's all she saw, and heard, and that
was the worst thing. All I remember is the tube
sticking out of my chest and then the doctor
arriving to remove it. *All done,* he said,

just a minor collapse, you shouldn't
have any further trouble.
I don't remember if he said *further,* or *minor,*
if he said *should* or *shouldn't.* All I remember
was *trouble,* he definitely said that,
and later when I asked Latika, she said
she couldn't remember either. And then paused
and said, *I think he said you'll be fine.*

The whine of the topdresser, closer and closer and finally appearing from behind the trees, changing pitch, a throaty roar, a sound she'd heard many times, but today there was wind and they had an agreement, they had an understanding, well, she wasn't sure Lewis understood but she thought he would stick to his word, her husband had helped him with mechanical issues and Lewis had received one of the first boxes of avocados, *It makes sense,* her husband had said, *keep your enemies close and all that,* a grin spreading across his face, and she had to admit that until then it had worked, but today an easterly, and there was the topdresser just visible about the trees pulling up and turning in a big arc, shutting off the jets too late, the fertiliser like fireworks sprayed up into the air, glinting in the sunshine and drifting on the wind over the trees and onto the bottom paddock, two months away from full certification, no room for error, no way this would fly, two months, she ran up to the house, shouting for her husband to get that idiot on the phone, her husband was on the porch rolling a cigarette and staring at her like a dumb animal as she ran past, straight for the hallway phone, there'd be hell to pay for this, hell to pay, and her husband said he'd thrown away his tobacco, that fuckwit, that fucking mother-fucking fuckwit, she took a breath, picked up the phone and dialled.

She was in a coma for three days, three days and three nights, a Bible story, a miraculous rising from the dead, but she didn't rise, and when the doctors were finally satisfied she woke to see the square panels of the ceiling, which she counted with her eyes until she registered her family on the periphery of her vision, slowly coming into focus, her daughters, the son, a few of their children, doctors, nurses, some in uniform, some like they just walked in from a family barbecue, no one she wanted to see, no one she wanted to see her, and then her husband, he spent more time than anyone, peering into her eyes, looking for something, something fertile to plant a seed into, but she wouldn't give it to him, she knew who he was, what he wanted, and she knew who she was, and who she was was different, not someone to be loved, someone to be feared, and she just needed to rest, she just needed to not move, not think about anything, not talk to anyone, she just needed to stare at the ceiling for a bit longer, *there's no rush,* she thought, *no sense in rushing when you've got nowhere to go and nowhere to be.*

The first viewing is a regional manager at Landcorp.
He's seen the numbers, wants to run a few tests.
How hard would it be to remove the avocado trees?
What did they farm here? A bit of everything.
They were certified biodynamic I say. The manager nods,
measures the width of the driveway, slowly taps
numbers into a tablet. The second is a flower grower,
sweeping, confident, her questions more like

someone getting into flower growing than someone
who knows what they're doing. I say my grandmother
originally wanted to grow flowers, which piques
her interest, but in the wrong way, a question
left hanging, unanswered. But she seems
impressed by the house, spends time
circumnavigating the verandah,
running her hand over the ornamental mouldings.
And the last guy doesn't say much,
just glances at the paddocks, the sky,
like he's trying to measure the distance,
like he can see something no one else can.
I ask him if he's from around here and he smiles.
I'm in construction, he says, scribbling
a final note in his leather folio, then
he slams it shut, zips it, and turns back to his car
like he's already made a decision.

Get your black hands off me, she said to the doctor, tried to stab
another patient with a butter knife, she battled with the nurses,
hollered and seethed, shrieked and muttered, eventually they
insisted on private care, *She's too disruptive,* they said, and her
husband took her home, a nurse came twice a week, but he had
to learn to dress her, bathe her, make her meals, manipulate
the food from the spoon into her mouth, and then when she
was asleep, find something to take his mind away, drive the
tractor, change the oil, watch *Coronation Street,* eventually he
started smelting lead in the garage, wheel weights, fishing
sinkers, forged whatever he could find into something new,
shapes in the dirt, a star, a cone, a leaf, the liquid poured in,

heavy, congealed and shiny as a mirror, like in that *Terminator*
movie, the bit where he crashes a truck and emerges from the
wreckage, the reflection of the fire sliding off him like water.

My thoughts disappear as I plough the top field.
I try to conjure up my grandmother
performing the same task, neatly unfurling
the rows, efficient, precise. And I realise
I only knew her as an adult, an elderly adult even.
Those earlier years, like crooked lines, a meandering
creek bed. When I'm finished, the field is a mess,
not a straight line anywhere. The earth ripped open
in large chunks, the field crisscrossed by tread lines.
I don't remember ripping a gash down the side
of the garage, corrugated iron torn open
like a cardboard box. Where was I? Did I black out?
I carefully back the tractor into the garage,
drop the plough onto the concrete with a bang;
the garage shakes. There's a gouge in the concrete.
On some summer evenings my grandparents
would let me sleep on the porch of this garage.
An old camp stretcher, a sleeping bag pulled up to my nose.
I wanted to see the stars. Richer and denser here
than at home. And I remember it
so clearly, the white concrete, green
roller doors, the pine framing underneath the roof,
cobwebs hiding in the corners. I remember it all
so clearly, except the stars. I don't remember
seeing any stars, and don't remember why.

Fruitless, the avocado trees dropped their leaves, overgrown with weeds, she lay in bed and moaned, her husband searched the internet for alternative medicine, radical overseas therapists, but really he wanted to be on his own for the first time in his life, be inside himself, and she did too, but in a different way, refusing to wear her dentures, refusing to eat without them, *She's, well, like a new person,* he said to his children, to soften the blow, but it was a lie, he couldn't remember who she used to be, the photos he leafed through were dead, like a slideshow of another family's holidays, he searched for old friends who were still alive, decided to join a sewing club instead, work on his precision, the things he'd never had time to perfect, eventually she stopped moaning and lay in silence, and he caught himself smiling when she told him to fuck off – *You fuck off,* he said, and he almost thinks he can see a smirk, a laugh, darting around behind her eyes, like something trapped.

The calendar is still there. Root days, leaf days,
flower days, and fruit. The moon explained, some theory,
how sap travels upward, in the ascendancy
and vice versa. The earth too, a metaphor, exhale, inhale,
exhale, inhale. But it's the line drawings
I remember the most, a glass of wine, some pumpkins,
beehives, chickens and pigs, a shovel in a pile of dirt,
a garden gnome with a fishing rod. The calendar
eleven years old and the weekdays falling on the same dates.
I run my finger over it – descending and waning,
sap sinking, the earth inhaling, water and fertilise,
plant and prune. Today, a new sign, cryptic, obscure.
It looks like a stylised set of buttocks? I read the key.

Libra, the flower day. It says on this day
the earth inhales. Whatever that means.
I turn the tap and drag the heavy body of the hose
over to the flower bed. A knot. I untangle it and there's
a sudden release, the nozzle whips across the grass
and I stand there watching it writhe and twist.

The phone alarm buzzes in my ear, I swipe it away
and throw the phone across the duvet.
Are you still in bed? It's 1pm.
I grab the phone, a blurry face fills the screen.
Sorry, I thought you were the alarm.
You set your alarm for the afternoon?
I reach for my glasses.
She looks energetic, on her lunch break,
probably up since six, getting the kids ready.
She asks how I am. *The farm is looking better.*
There's a couple of offers in already. I want to tell her
how the buyers seemed like idiots, will probably
ruin everything, how I've decided to visit
my grandmother, see her for myself,
but the words ball up in my throat.
I flop down, the phone hovering above me,
the muscles in my shoulder aching, and I can see
my image in the bottom corner, my face framed
by the baby-blue pillowcase and baby-blue sheets,
I turn my head to the side slightly and try a Hollywood pout.

She changed completely, almost overnight, one day a busy
suburban housewife, children recently left home, trips to

Queen Street, lunch at Fisherman's Wharf, shopping for shoes, and the next, in gumboots, shorts, digging holes with a spade, millet and nutritional yeast, daisy chains and glasses of milk, she gave away most of her things, only kept those pieces that reminded her of something, a hat, a dress, some pearls, possibly only worn on one occasion, a wedding, a night out at the Sapphire Room, the Hungry Horse, when her husband still held her hand, when her children still asked her questions, she kept a few pieces and forgot about the rest, gave them to charity shops, she was determined to be healthy, pure, unpoisoned, and she noticed she was changing too, she wasn't oblivious, *I'm just a more original version*, she said, *you're looking at the original, all that other stuff was weighing me down, I feel lighter,* and she meant it too, weeding the garden, lifting the sacks of chicken feed, turning the compost, she was lighter, freer, almost as light as the air, one day, in the autumn, the mornings beginning to cool, she could have sworn her feet hovered off the ground for a second, like she'd finally been released from it, untethered, before being drawn back again to that beautiful soil, her grubby sand shoes touching down again, imperceptible.

It's been decided. Everything will be sold,
or given away, even the clothes, the electric
organ, the old wingback chairs.
I make a petition to keep the organ
and my mother says I'm complicating things,
without explaining what exactly
I am complicating. I pack everything
into boxes and call the Salvation Army.
I leave a bed of course, and one chair,

a place to read at night, and a tall lamp with a frilly shade.
The new owners can figure out what to do with those.
I put any personal belongings in banana boxes –
photographs, jewellery, the diaries, keeping back
the ones I haven't read yet – then I fold up
the calendar and put that in the box too.
I decide no one will know if I hold on to
a couple of dresses, maybe a hat.
I fold them carefully and place them in my suitcase,
underneath my own clothes. I load everything
that's left into a trailer, borrowed from the charity.
Mostly junk, old crockery, furniture, a scratched
dining room table. When I go back into the house
I realise I'll have to clean it again. The dust,
the faded carpet, and when I'm done
it still smells like them, still looks like them,
the shadow of their lives still burned
into the walls, the carpet, the hardwood floors.

She occasionally let one out – a *shit* or even a *fuck* if the
occasion demanded it, like dropping a frying pan on your foot,
or a near miss in the car, she was raised on a farm after all – but
usually she was in complete control of her language, the way
she spoke, the letters that she wrote to friends, officials, family,
always measured and precise, and her husband, sort of the
same, although not precise, more like he'd drilled the words
into his mind many years ago, it was a kind of optimism, like if
someone threatened him or he made a mistake that might have
had dire consequences all he'd say was *gee whiz* or *shoot*, like
some kind of comic-strip school boy, and annoying as it was –

that he never got angry and lost control – it was also loveable, and in the beginning she had loved him for that too, loved how he was shocked when she suddenly lost it and let loose the full barrage, she wanted to say that she felt insulted by the universe more than anything else, insulted by herself and her inability to say what she really felt, a kind of frustration that just had to come out, and in the end he learned to wait it out, the return to normalcy coming soon enough, a half-hearted apology, a kiss, an awkward hand on the shoulder, but the apologies stopped eventually, and the kisses, although the hand on the shoulder remained, like a code for everything else, and after years of marriage, things repeating so many times, it didn't even feel like repetition anymore, it was just a kind of being, a daily event to add to the log before moving on to the next thing.

Latika sends me a follow-up text.
The kids and I will be there on Saturday.
They're driving me up the wall
and they need to see you too.
The day after the auction.
The day I should be heading back.
I'll have a few hours to see my grandmother
tell her what's going on with the farm,
make sure she's okay.
Latika doesn't say anything
about herself, or me, or us.
No *I love you* or *I can't wait to see you.*
But that feels okay. Not the right place, the right time.
I don't say anything either.
A final mow of the lawns.

I put away the two dishes I've kept
instead of leaving them on the rack, tidy my clothes,
quickly into the suitcase. It looks fine, people
like a project, like something they can instantly change.
And there's plenty of that. I take a walk round the boundary,
find a pile of rusting machinery under the pine trees.
It's hard to tell what it once was, a cylindrical part
and some pipes and square box, perhaps a pump,
or a small engine, it doesn't look that old, some green
paint still visible, but it does look discarded,
prematurely, like if I gave it a scrub
it might roar back into life. I hope someone sees it
during the pre-auction inspection and is won over
by the potential, decides to restore it,
the real thing just under the grass,
rusting, but still there. The people I've met
so far don't give me much hope.
They'll make rational decisions, calculations –
investment, profit, extraction, divestment. Inputs and outputs.
They can all see that the land is solid, that it will turn a profit
even if left fallow, so really, why do anything?
I'm reminded of a lecture at university
on economic value, the difference between use-value
and exchange-value, how there was no value system
for the environment that didn't include
how it could be used or exchanged. Or was it culture
or history that had no value? I can't remember
what course it was, or even which department,
but I do remember the lecturer, young and liberal,
he wore shorts every day, the kind of lecturer

I thought I'd be. There isn't any wind today.
Or if there is I'm sheltered from it beneath the pines.
I pull the clumps of grass back over the rusty machinery
and move on to where the beehives used to be,
the narrow corridor between the hedge and the chicken coop
where you had to walk slowly
so the bees could fly around you.

I read the last page of the diary, reading it backwards.
Last contact. She seems younger, rushed, her sentences
running into each other, chooks rushing in for a feed.
She was tireless, my mum told me. How she could never
keep up with her, a hint of resignation
in her voice as if she is still trying,
even though her mother
is staring at a TV in a care home.
And I feel like I'm lying, reading the diary.
This isn't her. This is a fiction, a story,
a bunch of words. And now
she's walking to the dairy in Gisborne, her mother
wants yeast and Epsom salts, she doesn't know
what those things are and forgets to get them,
returns home with a loaf of bread and some nectarines,
is rapped over the head for it. I'm beginning
not to believe a word of it.

They start to trickle in at about 12:30.
Some in fancy cars, one guy in a rusty ute.
The Landcorp man is back with his polar fleece
and a hatchback with advertising all over it,

a woman parks a Toyota Camry,
there's even a young couple in matching jeans
and a three-wheeled stroller
like they've just walked out of a Grey Lynn café.
The auctioneer stations himself on the verandah,
the bidders expected to arrange themselves
like a church congregation on the lawn.
The sunlight filters through the trees
and frames the auctioneer's face
as he looks down on us.
The garden looks good. I'm impressed with myself.
Bumble bees circle the flowers,
the heat of the day in full force.
Those without sunglasses shade their eyes
with their brochures and point at the trees in the distance.
Some talk in low voices, several look nervous,
others laugh in discreet fits.
I take up a place in the back, a little sad
to see it coming to an end, but mostly curious
about how it will work. The auctioneer calls them together
and the group falls silent. He explains the procedure.
Once the reserve is met, at the fall of the gavel,
the house is sold. If the reserve isn't met,
the vendor may decide to negotiate with the top bidder.
He implores everyone to bid if they want the place.
In a show of theatre, he clears his throat
and reads the description one more time,
embellishing it here and there with a few extra words
like *stunning* and *tailor-made*.
Finally he gets the auction underway,

starting at what seems like a high price.
He throws in a few more superlatives
to give people time to put their hands up.
Any starters? he says. *Starters at four point five?*
How about four? Three eight?
Mid-sentence, the hand of the woman
with the Camry shoots up.
The auctioneer points the gavel in her direction.
Can I get four? Three nine? The auctioneer
points toward the man with the rusty ute.
The woman immediately raises it to four. And again,
in an imperceptible movement, the rusty ute has the lead.
Now the café couple are involved, four point two,
but after one bid they're out. Now it's the Camry
versus the ute again. The bidding becomes furious.
They're up to five. The reserve still not met.
And the auctioneer reminds them of it,
like if they go faster the reserve will come down
to meet them. And then when the bidding starts to slow,
the auctioneer suddenly points to the side
and everyone turns to see who it is. The Landcorp guy.
The woman in the Camry is not letting go
and she doubles her effort, they're almost at six million.
The guy with the ute has given up, tucked his brochure
under his arm. *We've met reserve, ladies and gentlemen,*
says the auctioneer, and now everyone is turned toward
the woman with the Camry and Mr Landcorp, who don't even
look at each other as the bids gather. But Camry
begins to hesitate, Landcorp looks a little bored, like he's got
somewhere else to be. The auctioneer holds his arm straight

and direct at Landcorp. *Do we have any other bids?*
We have met reserve, ladies and gentlemen.
Last chance.
He makes eye contact with Camry.
Madam? Another five? She shakes her head. *Two?*
He draws it out with words and with the gaps in between.
This wonderful.
Property.
The farm you've always.
Going once.
Dreamed of.
Going twice.
He raises his gavel and holds it in the air for a long time,
and then just as he braces himself to bring it down,
he pauses and points his free arm toward the back.
A bid from the young man at the back.
I turn round to see the construction guy
entering from behind the hedge, his bidding hand
held up limply.
Six point two. Six. Point. Two. Million.
Sir?
Madam?
I look at my own wrinkled palm. It feels
like it's an old man's hand, like it belongs
to someone I've never met. I want to shout
Someone bid! Someone stop this from happening!
I turn my hand around, the knuckles
the ropey tendons narrowing at my wrist.
Surely this won't become another suburb,
a lifestyle hub, retirement village, surely

the land is worth something more.
I want to rush forward and pull his arm down, indicate
that it was a mistake. But that would look stupid,
or even like an act of fraud,
I feel dizzy. I look to Mr Landcorp,
the only chance of escape. I had no idea
I even cared who would buy this place,
but I can't control it, my system feels like it's wilting,
organs palpitating, my organs and nerves
don't know which way to send their signals.
He is shaking his head. *Are you sure sir? Last chance?*
Landcorp looks like he's never been more sure.
The writing on the wall. Progress. The economics,
marginal at best. He's seen all this before and is already
checking his watch. The auctioneer raises the gravel
high in the air and glances once more at Mr Landcorp.
He shakes his head and the gavel bangs hard
against cheap Formica. The sound rings in my ears
like a frying pan and a few birds screech and lift off
from a nearby tree, the bees seem to buzz
a few decibels louder. And then nothing,
I remember nothing more.

The constant news, a weak signal cutting out, intermittent,
every fifth word – *real, story, win, recommended, ethics, warnings*
– she doesn't hear it, the words, in the background like cicadas
popping their abdomens, the bulletins and the interviews,
irrelevant, the outside nonexistent, but talkback, real people,
with real problems, complaints, late at night, when the lines
have gone quiet, and a little light flashes on a board, *go ahead*

says the voice, exhuming, and the caller goes ahead, a twenty-minute argument against holistic medicine, all the years as a farmer's wife in one meandering rebuttal, the FM signal suddenly holds, like a window flung open, and she lies in bed listening to the words come and go, leaving their frail skeletons behind.

I leave the property for the first time since I arrived.
The stand of eucalypts slide away
in the rearview mirror and it feels like
I should take a last look, but as soon as it disappears
from view I catch myself glancing at the hat I've chosen,
a green pillbox with a thin chin strap.
Latika always says I suit green and I laugh
at the thought of her seeing me now and then
just as quickly that's gone with the thought
of her actually seeing me now. What would she say?
What would she do? At least she'll never know.
When I'm home. All this behind me. Real life.
The nursing home is at the edge of Pukekohe,
advancing, built only a few years ago.
I don't know why my uncles and aunties
chose this place. I guess they felt she should be close
to her own home, not that she would know,
not that she will ever get the chance to go back.
I pull into the large curved driveway,
the reception area, there doesn't appear to be
a spare park so I leave the car in a disabled space
in front of the door.

As she watched the trucks drive away – one half of the house on one truck, the other half on another, led off by a white ute with flashing lights and a wide load sign, another ute taking up the rear – she imagined one truck turning left and the other turning right, setting off for two different destinations, the house split forever, one going north for the warmth and the quiet life and the empty beaches and one going south for the cold fresh air, even more emptiness and the mountains in the background, a sense of scale, both aware of the other half not being there, but able to function anyway, a patched-up wall where the split used to be, repairing itself, thin, inarticulate, yet enough to continue, and she imagined them eventually forgetting each other, just being the house they are now; behind her are dozens of other houses in a bare dirt yard, hocked up on stilts so you could walk underneath, and that's what her husband was doing – curious, probably, about borer or the type of timber used, when he wandered back he said they should get going, so they slammed the doors on their little beige car and followed the trucks toward Pukekohe, *Do you think houses have a spirit?* she asked her husband, *No*, he said, *They're just timber, nails and iron*, she watched the street lights twinkle past and the empty motorway ahead of them, *but did you hear it creaking and groaning when they lowered it onto the truck, like it was talking*, her husband says nothing, concentrates on the road, the street light shadows yawning over his face, she keeps the conversation going in her head, *it knows it'll be a new house soon*, she thinks loudly, *similar but in a different environment, a different energy, a different house,* when they arrived just before dawn the trucks were struggling up the steep driveway, one was stopped on the final turn over the brow of the hill, unable to go forward or backward, locked inside the tight curve, and only after a lot of yelling and hand gestures – sliding backwards, lurching forwards and shuddery starts – did it finally make it to the top, and then the two halves were backed into place and lowered onto the foundations, and after the trucks finally left they stood under the slowly lightening sky and looked at their new home, uninhabitable, so much work still to be done, fixed to the foundations, sealing the roof, plastering, painting, a verandah, front steps, back steps, electricity, water, a septic tank, gravelling the driveway, garages, sheds, a chicken coop, and the garden, flowers, grass, trees, windbreaks, and standing in the mud, crisscrossed by ruts from the truck tyres, she smiled about the work, the future work, and with one hand she spun the cap off the thermos and poured them both a cup of tea to celebrate.

With her legs tucked out of the way,
my grandmother is lifted onto the ornate seat
of the old organ. It's an antique parlour organ
one of the care-home workers told me,
smaller than a piano, although higher,
reaching almost halfway to the ceiling.
While it is about as deep as a piano,
it's not as wide, a narrow little thing,
upright, like a toy, and my grandmother,
comparatively large, perched on the seat,
seeming to stretch up with it, unbuckling
the spine that's usually slumped to one side.
She pumps away with her feet, the air pressure
building until she releases it

with her fingers, evenly, fluidly.
And the loudness shocks me,
it's really loud, but not dark and majestic
like a church organ, like you'd think it would sound,
but thinner, lighter, more breathy,
like an accordion. And it's in my face
in that little room, it's louder
than the room needs it to be.
And even though she's playing a hymn,
moving her bony fingers over the keys,
her skinny body pumping away,
it sounds more romantic than spiritual,
like a French folk tune, sad and lonely.
The little tune starts
to burn its way into me.
I feel the sadness, the call
into the things we can never know.
I know relief will come if I just let a few
tears roll down my cheek, but I can't
do that here, so instead I close my eyes,
turn the music inward,
my lungs, the pump of the bellows,
the vibration, the air taken in
then expelled,
amplifying until it fills the room, which is
in its own unassuming way an amplifier too –
the pine, the soft furnishings, all part of the music,
arriving, leaving, breathing, waiting.
I open my eyes and the music has gone.
My grandmother is motionless

as if she was never really
playing at all, as if I imagined it.
She turns around, her eyes
staring straight at me, and this time
it's like the air has been sucked right out of her.

Fruit

She watches the kettle churn, shudder and hiss, the low rumble becoming a shriek as it nears boiling point, and just before it is about to shut itself off she jerks the plug from the wall, throws it to the side, narrowly missing the cup with its teabag waiting at the bottom, she turns to the window, watches the morning sun flicker through the trees, somewhere down the street a dog barks, a car rolls past, birds do their thing noisily in the trees, she grabs her bag and her shoes, shuts the door behind her, and on the doorstep she pauses, which way to go, she tries to imagine a destination, a purpose, something to aim for, but nothing comes, just the empty tea cup behind her, the dry tea bag, the silent kettle, the dead water, she decides to take one step and then another, down the path, out past the letterbox, and without thinking she turns left, toward Glenfield, she keeps on walking in the white heels she bought from the Postie catalogue, in the dress she bought on a shopping trip to the city, soft pink, wide across the shoulders, baggy sleeves, oversized chest pockets, cinched with a thick belt and tailored buttons, the collar up, brushing against her perm, peach button earrings, blue eyeshadow, she doesn't know why she is wearing all this, these clothes are not comfortable, she could have put on some tennis shoes and slacks, anything else, she doesn't know where she's going, doesn't know why, she just walked out the door with no intention other than to leave, go somewhere, out of the house, out of Birkenhead, out of the city, out of New Zealand, out of 1987, and now the sun is shining, and the footpath clear, and her head is clear too, or beginning to clear, and she walks up Onewa Road toward the shops, the dairy, the hairdresser, the post office, and the garage she recently owned with her husband, *under new management*, another banner plastered over that, *opening soon*, she looks to the other side of the street, she remembers the children coming in after school, raiding the drinks fridge, playing out the back in the piles of tyres, and later, after they learned to drive in one of the rental cars, serving customers, collecting fish and chips for the weekend workers, or late at night, the kids asleep, she and her husband having a beer with the mechanics after a particularly long Friday night shift, relaxed, the way they were with each other when all the work was done, but that's all gone now, the mechanics working elsewhere, the kids all left home, grandkids, and as soon as the business was sold her husband booked a trip to Europe, the awkward conversations they had about him taking his mother, how she could come if she wanted, but they both knew that wouldn't be possible, and now the new management moving in, taking over, making new memories, their own mistakes; at the intersection

of Birkenhead
Avenue,
she waits to cross to the sunny side, and while she's there,
motionless, a moment of hesitation, maybe she should just
go back to the flat and put her pyjamas back on, what is she
thinking, she really does have nowhere to go, no purpose, she's
dressed for a party but there's no party here, no people, not
even a car, just a dog sleeping outside the dairy, the hum of a
transformer nearby, the light turns green and she crosses the
road, mostly by rote, and she finds herself on the other side,
walking, embarrassed at the thought of someone seeing her stop
and hesitate and turn around, overdressed, erratic, some crazy
old person lost in her own neighbourhood, she keeps walking
down the road as if she has somewhere to go, as if she isn't lost,
one step at a time, one step at a time, and eventually she starts
the long climb toward Glenfield, the top of hill, the view that
she knows is there, the perspective she knows she needs;
for a while,
she's been feeling
that something isn't
right, inside,
inside her body,
her mind,
inside,
inside,
get inside,
like there's a poison setting in, or maybe some element that's
missing, something vital that she's not getting as she should,
her environment, maybe her food, and this is what is making
her sick, making her lose weight, making her fret and stay in

bed all day, wondering what could have been, so she tells her daughters, and they laugh, her life is so good, what does she have to complain about, retirement, a good profit from the sale of the business, *take it easy,* they say, *that's all you need, stop worrying,* they don't get it, they don't really listen, although they never have, so why would she expect them to start now, though her husband is much better, not because he doesn't listen but because he doesn't think like that, he is always addressing the thing right in front of him, it has to be obvious for him to see a problem, but then if he does see it he will fix it, but this is something more subtle, more fluid, something you can't fix with a spanner or a hacksaw, as she passes the rugby fields and the RSA she wonders what he is doing now, if he's in some quaint English pub in the Midlands, where supposedly his family is from, but probably not, he's never really been a drinker, half a pot of beer on the weekend, his limit, limited appetite for socialising, too busy working, too busy fixing, resolving, inventing, profiting, and as far she knows, he never went to the Northcote RSA, or any RSA for that matter, never went for the cheap beer or for the Sunday roast, a round of darts, it sounded all right to her, but he never even mentioned it as a possibility, and he never mentioned the war either, the years just before they met, you'd think it might have come up but it never did, not in any detail, and sometimes he would look at her in a particular way, sometimes on a silent night while they were eating or reading, he would sigh quietly and she knew he was resenting her a little, resenting her for not providing something he had over there, and what that was, she could only guess, maybe it was shameful, maybe it was just youthful, but whatever it was, for all these years, it sat between

them like a stranded hulk;
her heel
is rubbing
on the inside of her shoe, her Achilles tendon, the beginning
of something, but she's got a rhythm going now and continues
on past cemeteries and more houses, and she reaches the
entrance to the Birkenhead Domain, where the flood of native
bush races down the hill into a small valley, a stream, and then
connects to the reserve, following the stream for kilometres,
preserved, cherished by the community, it's a place she has
enjoyed since she moved here, since her husband left on his
trip, a place she doesn't feel quite so alone, even though she
rarely meets anyone, she pauses and adjusts her foot inside
her shoe slightly, jamming it forward, she crouches down and
tightens the strap, and when she stands up she almost feels
like turning left and plunging headfirst into the domain, but
today is not the day for blundering about in the bush, she
feels like she needs to go somewhere new, something with
a clear direction, a goal, a beginning and an end, and as she
takes up the pace again, the rubbing on her heel settles down,
and she turns her back on Birkenhead, continues along the
ridge, noting the street signs as she leaves them behind, Park
Road, Roberts Road, Capilano Place, she doesn't look back
over her shoulder, the North Shore stretching out toward the
harbour and Auckland proper, neither does she look over the
other shoulder toward the upper harbour, the marshland, the
shallow bays and mangroves, she doesn't really think about
what is behind her at all, instead, what will she find if she
keeps walking in this direction, has she ever been on this road
before, beyond the mall, the suburbs, the bleeding edge, has

she ever had a reason too, what was she waiting for, and who is this person, she never used to be confined, in Gisborne, as a young woman, before business and back aches, before this little suburb in this big city, she had the whole country back then, from Māhia to Urewera, to Whakatāne and even Hicks Bay, the world was large and unfenced, unroaded, and she travelled easily, by foot, bicycle, horseback and her father's car, and then her husband arrived, a car, a career, a child, and then they moved for financial reasons, fashionable reasons, a lack of dissenting reasons, and that's how, without her realising it, her world became small, not metaphorically or psychologically small, but physically small, her small house, her little garden, her tiny television, everything she needed was immediately accessible, there was no reason to go anywhere else, and now she's walking, leaving behind, shedding, she can feel flakes of anxiety falling, littering, melting into the hot asphalt, and she walks past the villas and bungalows, their high fences and old trees, and then the state houses with wide open lawns and tiny citrus trees, a different aesthetic but just as romantic, and townhouses, built recently, filling the spaces in between, some of them in the style of farm houses, rows of steeples and stable doors, Jacuzzis and carports, she feels their familiarity, even though she might never have looked at that particular house before, particular fence, particular tree, she knows them, but there's no one around today, no open doors, no children, no elderly, everyone at work or school or shopping or sleeping, only the odd car lazily rolling down the hill and then whirring out of earshot, only her own footsteps and the general buzz of insects and some distant city noise, the road is long and straight and wide and slightly rising, which gives her a sense of purpose, she focuses on the furthest point she can and strides toward that, the progress is slow, and the gradient of the road increasing slightly, rising, until she reaches the point she saw earlier, what she thought was the crest of the rise, and the horizon flattens out again, in the distance, the road steepens into a rise, a new edge, edges on top of edges, and it suits her, this slow stepped hill, every rise a new goal to aim for, focus on, satisfy, and the minutes and miles float past, she barely notices them, counting only the number of goals achieved, relishing their increasing difficulty and her increasing tiredness, using that to push harder, ignoring the pain in her heel that has spread to the top of her foot and the lump on the outside of her little toe, using the pain, form and rhythm, minimising it, not stopping, she knows it could mean the end of her expedition, starting harder than stopping, eventually she rounds a long sweeping corner, a triangular patch of grass between the main road and a side road, the houses thin out, and she knows where she is, the peak, the top of the hill, from here on a slow descent toward the mall, but she finds this harder, gravity now on her side and not something to fight against, there's no goal now, she just has to succumb to it, and she starts to feel the weight of her legs, the difficulty of lifting them for every step, she scuffs her foot and almost trips on a slightly raised piece of concrete;

she's tired,

she notices

she's tired,

why not take a break at the mall, she thinks, *a cup of tea, a scone or something,* if she makes it that far, she can always catch the bus home, maybe do a bit of shopping beforehand, watch a movie, that sounds nice, and she starts to accelerate down the hill, a new flood of energy, heels clipping the asphalt, she looks down on the featureless building of the mall, no indication of what's inside except for the few tantalising shop signs dotted around the outside, 1 hour dry-cleaning, Bernina, Quaggs Ice Cream Parlour, Majestic Wines, but she knows it's when you enter through the sliding doors that the mall really comes to life, with its continuously running escalators, women dressed up and towing shopping bags, children, friends, up and down, down and up, it's inside that the place advertises itself, like entering another world, cool and well lit, it's a shock to the body to pass through those doors, to move from the open sky, the rows of cars in the carpark, the smell of pollen and petrol fumes, and to break through, the smell of vacuum-sealed packaging and perfume, she looks down on the mall and the carpark already mostly full and hurries down the zigzagging path to the main entrance;

inside,

get inside,

she heads straight for the café and orders a cup of tea and a chocolate lamington, she eases her shoes off and rubs her feet, she can see red marks on the top and the beginnings of a blister on her heel, she puts the shoes back on and waits for her tea, it tastes wonderful, and the lamington is soft and fluffy with plenty of whipped cream and it's not long before there's only a few crumbs left, which she picks up on the end of a wet finger and places on her tongue, after she's finished she starts to feel tired, like her body wouldn't get up even if she wanted to, catching a movie, shopping, catching the bus home is more effort that she can be bothered with, or not much effort, but boring, repetitive, like she can imagine doing those things and then going home and being unable to recall what movie she saw, what she bought, where she bought it from, and if someone asked she would just shrug and say the walk was nice, I don't know about those movies, but the walk was nice, and maybe that's what she should do, keep walking, keep going toward the opposite of easy, her body is tired, but how far can it go, how far could she push it, what's beyond the mall, she's not sure she's ever been past it, not sure what's on the other side, her body doesn't feel so lethargic anymore, maybe the tea and sugar, maybe something else, either way she should use it and use it now, so she stands up quickly, down the escalator, past the photo developing shop, the menswear, the womenswear, the shoe shop, where her eyes are drawn, but she keeps walking, and she sees the sunlight through the glass doors ahead, and as she approaches the doors slide open to let someone else come in and she speeds up because she can make it before they close again, *Hi,* someone says loudly and she turns round, and several other people turn toward to the voice too, everyone seems to be looking at everyone else, and then she sees Margaret, waving her hand up high so she can be seen over the people between them, *I thought that was you,* Margaret says as she pushes through the crowd, breathing hard, *I thought that must be you, and it was,* people nearby pretend not to look, *fancy a cup of tea?* she asks, smiling, Margaret is her husband's second cousin, she doesn't say anything and Margaret keeps talking, *How about lunch? Caprice?* but she tells Margaret as politely as she can that she has to head home, without committing to what exactly she has to head home for, Margaret doesn't look disappointed and then she is gone, diffusing into the shopping centre, and she takes the opportunity to leave herself;

outside,

a deep

breath,

outside,

unaware

that she is holding on to it, holding it in, and it all comes rushing out in one big sigh, her shoulders and chest, and the air rushes back into her lungs, filling, she straightens, looks left, looks right, one way leads back to Birkenhead, the other, not back to Birkenhead, and decides to continue on down Glenfield Road, go as far as her feet will take her and then catch a bus or call a taxi to get home, and she likes this plan, the one-wayness of it, she takes one step forward, then another, her feet and legs definitely heavier than when she started, but less heavy than when she stopped at the mall, *I'll walk until the energy from the lamington runs out,* she says to herself under her breath, and then under that too, she says it again, as though someone else is talking inside her head, she continues with the words replaying in her mind *until the lamington runs out, until the lamington runs out, until the lamington,* and before long the mall is behind her, she is exiting the valley, climbing again, another ridge road, another hill, the corner just up there, the road cresting, unseen beyond, and then as she approaches she can see that it flattens out, that she's walking on top of the ridge and she can see the North Shore stretching out to her right, Rangitoto in the distance, its long sloping shoulders always closer than they should be, lazy, dominating, and all the houses, construction, parks and tree-lined valleys in between the island and her seem insignificant, all she can see is the scarred green body of the dormant volcano, a monument to unpredictable violence, it gives her chills, something like that, always looming, over there, she picks up the pace, the gradient is easier and she looks directly ahead, head high, focused on the next waypoint, a lamp post, an odd-shaped tree, forgettable things, made more important just by being next, and then one final long slope along the ridge, the houses falling sharply away on either side of the road, her energy suddenly wanes, some battery inside her depleted, reserve power, her pace slows until she's reduced to a shuffle, the tiniest steps she can manage while still moving forward, and like this she creeps up the hill, a white water-tower at the top, she focuses on that, and slowly it becomes larger and larger, until she can make out its curved sides and corrugated-iron roof, and as she nears it she realises it's not curved but made from narrow flat panels, ten-sided, sixteen, maybe more, and staked into the grass, a sign, *keep out*, she crosses a side road and stands in front of it, feet aching, the tank looming in front of her, and she imagines it filled to the top, all that weight, all that water, waiting for someone to turn on a tap down in the valley, the water rushing out through a network of pipes and mains, hissing through valves;

she decides

to take a break,

to decide

what to do

next –

climbs over the low railing, ignoring the sign, she leans up against the water tank, slips her shoes off, a raw patch of blood on both heels, blisters formed and already broken, maybe this is it, she thinks, as far as I can go, I can knock on a door and ask someone to call me a taxi, or I can hitchhike, this idea makes her happy, satisfied that she's done enough, she stands up to look for a house where someone is likely to be home, some sign of life, perhaps they'll spare her a glass of water, there is a ladder on the side of the tank and she starts to climb, the roof of the tank gently slopes to a central point and she clambers up to the highest part and stands up, the countryside is open before her, the tank marks the edge of the city, on one side rows of houses, people inside them doing homely things, and on the other side miles of farmland, only the odd house visible, a long sloping valley, and in the distance sharp hills, etched with valleys and draped in dark green trees, pine trees she presumes, she looks from the city to the country, from order to chaos, from boredom to freedom, she feels nauseous on top of the water tower, she crouches and places one palm on something solid, and this makes her feel even more unsteady, she closes her eyes and takes a breath and that helps a little, she takes another, opens her eyes and climbs down off the water tower, throwing her shoes onto the grass before she climbs down the ladder, and back on the ground, the view of the city and countryside hidden behind bushes, she feels better, the nausea disappearing as quickly as it came, she recovers her shoes, *I'll keep going,* she thinks, *why would I go back now, I've still got the whole day ahead of me,* she looks down at her bloodied heels, *I can walk on the verge, it'll be nice to have the grass between my toes, there's no one to stop me,* she looks around, half expecting someone to step out and stop her, but no one appears, the road is silent, the houses silent, only the bush in the distance seems to make a noise, like wind, but not really that, a hum, just humming, impersonal, indifferent, saying go or don't go, I

don't care, this way or that way, it's up to you, she drinks from a
tap she finds on the side of the tank, then starts walking again
with a shoe in each hand, the road mostly downhill, she finds
it easy and almost pleasant, long kikuyu grass thickly matted
on the side of the road, she passes farmhouses, the odd patch
of bush, gravel driveways, letterboxes with little metal flags
either up or down, orchards, sheep paddocks, small industrial
operations of some kind, a row of plastic-caped hothouses,
another water tank, a golf course, what looks like a cemetery
through the trees, a rubbish fire behind a hill, the smoke rising
and disappearing, and on she walks, her legs and feet numb,
but her mind disengaging, and it's easier to keep going than to
stop, in her head, easier to stay still by continuing, the rhythm
of her feet, the slight tug of the descent, the change of scenery,
the air somehow cooler than in the suburbs, and she breathes in
the smell of soil and grass and burning leaves, and in her ears,
the hum of the bush, she turns a corner and the air crackles
and buzzes, powerlines high above the road, over the fields,
before lifting, arcing up, and over, the hills, she walks around
the corner and behind a high barbed-wire fence, power boxes,
ceramic insulators, scaffolding, poles, bridges and arches, and
as she nears it the buzzing increases, she is right underneath
the lines and right next to the substation, and it feels like she's
inside a forcefield, behind a waterfall, the energy envelops her,
she's comforted, she's inside it, but then another sound pushes
through the curtain, intrusive, an engine, a car engine, low and
heavy, rumbling around the corner, the driver puts their foot
down and the car accelerates, the rumble turning into a hard
clacking sound, and then, just as suddenly, it drops away with
a little burp and the car is rumbling again, and she can feel

it approaching through the hairs on the back of her neck, the driver gives it another burp with the clutch in, for show, and it's loud now, right behind her, she can hear the stones fighting to get out from under the tyres;

she starts walking,

almost running, but not quite, don't show fear, keep moving, she leaves the halo of the substation, passes the handful of worker's cottages that circle it, back among the gorse and dust and dry stormwater ditches, and the car is closer, she can hear laughter, more than one voice, she is walking, not running, but she knows the cat is out of the bag now, they can tell she's afraid, that she's trying to avoid them, but she won't run, like that's what this is all about, all this, just to make her run, panic, give in completely and run, and they'll laugh if she does that, and they'll win, so she picks up the pace, her thighs burning with the strain of not being able to run, they are alongside her, another loud burp when they drop behind a little, she wants to turn to see their faces, but she can't without stopping and swivelling right round, so she keeps a steady pace, looking straight ahead, hoping they become bored, but after a few minutes they haven't left, and as she rounds the next corner the gorse turns to pine forest, tall trees, closing in on the road, and for the first time her determination starts to waver, this is not a good place to be, she's going in the wrong direction, and she can't help it, like she's being swept along with the thrumming of the engine, like an undertow, being pulled somewhere she doesn't want to go, and this is all part of the plan, and she's falling right into it, she considers running, unlocking herself and letting fly, suddenly, unexpectedly, full commitment, perhaps back to one of the workers' cottages, they won't expect that, it'll take them a minute to turn around, she'll get a head start, she might just make it, but what are the chances anyone will be home, maybe she could leap the fence and hoof it into the forest, probably her best option, but then she'd be far from the road, far from help, and surely another car will come by soon and she can wave them down, but no car comes, and the solitude she had been enjoying all day now feels dangerous, and she longs for someone, anyone, to appear, she reaches into her handbag for the pencil that she knows is there, always kept sharp, she slides it into her palm, the point against her wrist, her thumb over the eraser on the end, she keeps her hand inside the bag so they won't know what she has in there, she swivels her engagement ring so that the sharp stone is pointing straight out, and the car rumbles on, round one corner and then another, clacking as it pushes up a small slope, and then idles down the other side, she hears laughter again, someone swearing, she keeps walking, slowing down a little now, she's not sure how long this can go on for, what are they doing, either do something or leave, the stupidity of it, she crunches her knuckles together until they turn white, tensing her arm, shoulder, chest, pit of her stomach, unable to stop the anger flooding in, resistance of bone and muscle, she grits her teeth, and feels like turning and charging straight at them, a show of deranged aggression, but the more she considers it, the less likely it seems to happen, so she keeps walking, tense and alert, and just as she really is about to turn and say something – *What do you want?* or *Go away*, or something like that – the engine roars, someone yells out the window, *You'll keep bitch*, the car slews sideways, spitting gravel, straightens and accelerates over the hill and round the corner, dust spewing from the wheel wells, and finally it's out of sight, she can hear the engine chewing through the gears, the dust settles back on the road, she gasps, sucks in air, the pencil still clutched in her fist, her breath still trapped in her chest, she looks round to see if anyone is watching and then she jumps the fence, runs for the pines, over logs and under low branches, through the brush, weaving through the tree trunks, the forest becoming denser, her toes digging into the pine needles as she runs, and even though the trees are in columns and rows, a grid, there is no road to follow, no path, no A to B, just endless trees, ordered and meaningless, she keeps moving and at some point senses she is deep in the forest, the light dimmer, her eyes adjust, definitely darker, she looks behind her and can't see the road, or any sign of the road, she stops and crouches down behind a trunk;

definitely darker,

definitely,

deep breaths,

dark breaths,

definitely,

she tries to unfurl her mind, disentangle it from the blood in her ears, there's no sign of the car returning, just silence, she takes deeper breaths, through her mouth and her nose, and finally calms a little, her pulse slows, she can feel it, and she can think, she can't go back to the road, she listens for any sound, but there's none from that direction, just the faint hum, the whisper, behind her, up in the treetops, up on the ridge, she turns to face it, she can't see anything, but she listens, and it's there, it doesn't sound like wind, it doesn't sound like water;

she starts to move

toward it,

at first she finds it easy, a soft loamy bed of pine needles, a gentle slope and the odd slightly steeper section, steps made from the tree roots, she keeps up a good pace, almost marching, the damp soft earth on the soles of her feet, caked in mud but strong and light, every muscle from her toe to her neck working together to propel her further from the road, further up the hill that has begun to steepen, the trees crowding in a little more, sometimes she has to shimmy sideways, look ahead for an easier route, doubling back if she's blocked by a fallen branch or a section that's too steep, but she doesn't feel lost, despite not knowing where she is, she knows where to go, towards the hum, up the hill, and she feels stronger, more confident in where she is going, the hill becomes steeper and the trees less gridded, less straight, often gnarled and bent now, and her confidence rises, she doesn't bother finding the easiest route, it's now a scramble, finding a path wherever she can, using her arms to pull, her feet, on all fours sometimes, her foot slips and she cracks her shin on a rock, she rips her dress on a broken lower branch, she doesn't even think to look back, she hauls herself up, it feels good to use her arms, her legs in harmony, and her back, a full-body effort just to get to the next tree root, more difficult, more determined, she can't see more than a few metres in front, no idea what is behind her, not caring what is behind her, she climbs and climbs, her arms stronger as she goes, as if the exertion is fuel for the exertion;

she reaches a small rock outcrop

and barely slows down, finds a good handhold, tests it then hauls herself up, she finds a solid place for her foot and pushes, reaching for the next handhold, she pulls, she arches and contorts her way up the rock face, when she reaches the crest she realises this was just the first part, there's a small ledge carpeted in pine needles, and above that another ledge, she wipes her hands on her hips and reaches up, pulling and pushing, testing the strength of the rock, testing herself, her fingers reaching for handholds, finding them, one continuous motion, one continuous effort, and then she's on top of the rock, above her are more roots, more rocks but steeper and crumblier, the roots less anchored, she looks back and imagines how she might reverse and clamber back down, but how would she do it, slowly lower her body down rather than pulling herself up, she'd have to look for footholds, search around for them blindly, what if her foot doesn't find one, what if the grip isn't good, what if she slips while going down, she would fall instantly, her other limbs would be partially engaged, they'd be lowering, not lifting, weak not strong, there'd be no chance for her other limbs to take up the slack, she looks up again, no, the only way is up, the only way,

she tests a root and it breaks away in her hand, kicks a rock and it crumbles into gravel, another, the ledge isn't so fissured, it holds the weight of her foot, she finds a thicker root, it doesn't budge and she pulls herself up, slowly, finds a rock for her other hand, a root for her foot, she tests out hold after hold and makes her way higher, she starts to recognise which roots will be strong and which pieces of rock are less weathered and her progress speeds up, she looks up and can't see the end, but she knows there is a top to this hill and she can't be that far from it, so she keeps going, there is no way back, there is no good answer, her muscles are feeling good, her arms, her legs, she can feel them, they are working, but they feel strong like they want more work, like she will have to concentrate to slow them down, take care, and she does, picking her way up the slope and she feels like she's almost there, almost at the end, she doesn't know why but she can feel this and maybe this last solid root as thick as her wrist will be the final pull and she'll be up and over, so she grips it firmly and pulls herself up, at the same time her left foot reaches for the foot hold that she can see is solid and perfectly placed, and then her arm is weightless and there is nothing to pull against, the root has broken or perhaps it was never attached, and she's been too hasty, and gravity is pulling her back, dread is pulling her back, what have you done, where are you going, where have you been, she closes her eyes and waits for the inevitable, and her other foot slips and she spins around facing outward from the cliff, spinning back, a strange muted squeak comes out of her mouth as her arm burns and twists and threatens to let go, but it holds and eventually her momentum turns her back round and facing the cliff again, her feet scrabble at whatever they can find, sending scree down the slope, eventually one foot finds half a root, enough to take some of her weight and she looks down for a place for her other foot, there's a thin root stronger than it looks and she's stable, panting, gasping, the one that saved her, burning, and she lets the weight go off it, giving it a break, deep breaths, slowly coming back to what's next, rather than what's now, she looks up, her arms stretched above her, long, desperate, refusing to let go;

and she notices the sinew,

the long ropey tendons and muscle,

the arms others always admired, when they noticed the lumps on her shoulders, her biceps and the tangled muscle around her forearm, almost like a man's arms, although no one ever said that, but she could tell they thought it, when she said this to her husband, he laughed, and said he loved her man arms, and she believed him, she knew he admired her for lots of reasons, she could tell when people faked admiration, but in a moment of self doubt she wondered if there was something else going on underneath, if sometimes he wished he was married to a delicate flower he could take care of and protect, someone he had to be careful with, someone who couldn't exist on their own, who needed him to exist, when she thought about this she had to tell herself that she was all things at once, she was delicate and strong, people were complex, people were different every day, as soon as you had someone pegged they were unpegged, we all have patterns but we also have anti-patterns, and then she realised he probably never wondered what she thought of him, and that was enough to bring her back to the world, back to the slope, what was next, and she can feel it, she is close, achingly close, so she stretches her fingers, her neck strains, and the stretch runs from her skull to her fingertips, she feels the power and youth returning to her body in a wave, a big surge, youth and strength and power, like everything she has ever done has led towards this moment, and she heaves herself upward, an elbow, a knee, she scrambles and pulls and pushes, but always forward, no doubt now, and then she's there, she's made it, there's no more, she flops down on the flat rock, weirdly smooth like a table, and she could be somewhere else, Gisborne, or India, or back home in her bed, the musty woollen blanket, the cold floor, her slippers on the other side of the room, so she'll stay here, her body heavy like rock, her brain firing in all directions, and her body with no

direction at all,
and then the smell,
electrical wires,
burning,
definitely the smell of wires, she tries to roll over, but her left
arm is lifeless, her left leg too, she looks up and there's a weird
tunnel with the sky in it, she can't see anything on the sides,
it's a black tunnel, a disc of blue sky, she reaches for her face
and it feels like it's slipping off,
she can't feel her own hand touching her own face, she tries
to call out for help but something garbled comes out,
like someone else trying sounds on for size,
random, confused, a baby trying them on for size,
then stuffing them in her mouth
like socks, burning wires,
slipping off, garbled,
random, a baby,
her left arm,
her mouth,
a blue disc,
a black square,
diamonds,
kettles boiling,
blue bottles,
white milk,
a newborn baby
staring up at her.

Aka Aka Road is fast and straight
with a couple of ninety-degree corners
to throw you off. I leave my lights on
high beam, the road racing beneath me.
I peel down the window and humid air rushes in,
hotter than the air inside the car,
and I'm thinking about what I should say
when I see Latika, will something sweet
and funny come to me, like it used to
when we first met and our conversation
was so easy and she laughed a lot
and she made me laugh, when we talked about our families
and our childhoods, our favourite TV shows.
Or will it die before it even begins, a hug,
something about the drive and the luggage in the boot,
that I should get everything in before it rains.

It could go either way. Any way.
Like a first date, it might burn with promise
or be nothing at all.

Road signs tell me the on-ramp is near
and the road widens into two lanes,
small clumps of flax appear,
a cycle lane and large stormwater drain
and I can hear the shuddery hum
of the motorway. Another sign indicates
I should stay left for north,
right to go south. I can hear a crackle
in the distance, and a smell, something alive,
something burning, about to change,
and suddenly the whole sky flashes –
I see everything in front of me,
every stone, every fleck of paint, every flax,
every flower, from Mangere to the Bombay Hills.
Brilliant white. Like when you flick on the light
over the bathroom mirror first thing in the morning.
Your pale eyes and lips.
And then as quickly as it came
it's gone, and the darkness returns
and the rain starts to fall.

I flick the indicator arm with my index finger,
glance in the rearview mirror and catch
the corner of an old eye, shadowed,
the skin around the edges crinkled
and dry, and the colour of the iris

still there, still grey, staring back at me
like an animal, cold and wild.
The animal blinks and I change
from the lane I don't want to be in
to the one I do.

Acknowledgements

Many thanks are due to the people who read earlier drafts and encouraged me along the way. Especially Lynn Jenner, Lawrence Patchett, Tina Makereti, John Summers, Sarah Jane Barnett, Rachel O'Neill and Alison Glenny.

To Ashleigh Young, Fergus Barrowman, Todd Atticus, Anna Knox and the rest of the THWUP team for making this book better.

To Robin Robertson and Mike McCormack for writing radical novels and providing runway lights for the final approach.

To Biodynamics New Zealand and the Soil Association UK for helping with the research.

To Mum for answering questions about the family. To my extended family, both old and new, and no longer with us. Many of you appear in fictional form throughout this book. I hope you get a kick out of that.

To the city of Edinburgh and the town of Pézenas for the background noise. To Auckland, both north and south, for always being in the foreground.

To Creative New Zealand for creating the time to finish this.

To Gerard Duignan for getting me off the mountain that night. And to the incredible staff of Wellington Hospital and the Brain Injury Clinic. I don't remember it but I bet it was spectacular.

And the most loving thanks to my partner, Lindsay Carlyle, for so many incompressible reasons.